A COLLECTION OF SHORT STORIES

EDITH SANDERS

EDITH SANDERS PUBLISHING

FOREWORD

Born and brought up in Greenock, where she lives with her husband, both now retired. After a working life in Banking and Local Government, she returned to the Writers' Club in 2016, after a break of several years. Writing provides a challenge, whether it be a Story, an Article, a Poem or a Competition Entry. She has her name on a few of the club trophies and certificates. Also a member of the Greenock Art Club, painting in mediums such as Water Colour, Pastels or Acrylic. As a member of Greenock Lady Speakers' Club, she frequently makes her voice heard.

"It is all about keeping the Little Grey Cells in working order"

CARRY ON MOTORING

I step forward and kneel in front of the King. He smiles as he places the Order of the Tolerant Navigator (Motor Vehicle Division), around my neck.

He whispers a sympathetic "Well done! It is not easy being the navigator is it."

I stifle a polite titter.

My better half demands to know why I am laughing. "I nodded off and I was dreaming."

"Hmm. Well ... pay attention to the signs."

I nod wearily, thinking to myself that there should be an award for all the long-suffering wives and girlfriends who have had the dubious pleasure of acting as navigators to their own special male.

I am sure that there must have been an award in past centuries. Imagine the scene in Roman times when man took woman for a ride in his new chariot.

"Turn left at the Forum," she instructs.

"It's a one-way street, did you knot see the sign?" he bellows. Familiar words in the battle of the sexes.

My train of thought rumbles on. What would the award

look like? It's for a female, so perhaps a red ribbon with a small gold map hanging from it, or a small glove or sports car? Earrings to match? No. I don't think so! I laugh aloud.

"Glad you find something funny. Hmm. Columbus would never have discovered America if you had been his navigator."

I seethe, silently. Yes, we are on holiday again. We are *touring the Continent*. that phrase to me conjures up the glamorous hey-days when the rich just managed to find their way to the south of France – after a 'frightful' journey, of course.

I can see myself in the white convertible something-or-other type car, expensive, low and sleek; my hair flying in the wind, my husband beside me urging the chauffeur to step on it and get us to Monte in time for dinner.

IN MY DREAMS!

I return to reality. A navigator's job is to navigate, which I do. To speak or not to speak, that is the question: whether it is necessary to give instructions or to engage in light and pleasant conversation.

It is also my wifely duty to fill the glove compartment and any other hiding places with emergency rations of polo mints, barley sugar and chocolate.

Tapes, CDs and the mobile phone are to be squirelled away in yet another place. After all that, if we did break down on some remote mountain pass, the St Bernard with the brandy would find us: but there's not much chance of that on the M6!

My thoughts drift forward to our destination – a week of sheer pleasure in The Cotswolds.

We are now passing through Broadway, a village of chocolate-box beauty and an air of times past. I can just imagine the stagecoach stopping at the Broadway Hotel and the passengers stepping down, and into the comfort of the tavern.

We turn into a quiet country road, which I am sure in the olden days must have been patrolled by highwaymen. A few more seconds and we stop at Buckland Court.

This little hamlet always seems to suddenly appear in all its honey-coloured glory, like a sort of Brigadoon. I can't wait to get into our comfortable, well-furnished cottage, our home from home.

I realised a long time ago that our car and myself are under the strict command of the driver at all times. Air conditioning or heating are regulated by him. Touching anything unless told to do so is a bit of a 'no-no' and fiddling in my handbag is definitely frowned upon.

However we have arrived safely and yes there is still a welcome tray. It is such a kindly gesture and makes for instant relaxation as we sit down with a cuppa.

A little later, unpacking finished.

Now it's time to settle, put the "instants" in the microwave. OPEN A BOTTLE OF WINE!!

There is nothing like food and wine to soothe the savage breast.

My better half becomes himself again ... So, who was in the car with me all day?

The tension eases, we are talking again, and "he who must be obeyed" denies all knowledge of tempers becoming frayed as the day progressed.

The Italian grape is seducing his senses and he admits, "Yes, I did see one or two people who seemed to be arguing, quite amusing really."

Amusing? I find it comforting to look around when we stop for petrol or whatever, and to see fellow travellers with the same strained looks and hear the same raised voices.

We plan the outing for the next day. I agree. Yes, I will pay attention, give instructions in plenty of time, etc. etc. I'm just the navigator and I do my best, admittedly on a shortish fuse.

I know my personal driver is an understanding man with an abundance of patience: I know I prattle on urging him to look at this and that as we drive along: I also give him the historical lowdown on the next stopping-place. What's wrong with that?

Maybe he does have an excuse for being a little grumpy. That being the case, surely my day-dreaming on the boring parts of the motorway is essential therapy for the navigator.

It helps to blunt the verbal slings and arrows fired by the driver!

Tomorrow is another day, new places to see. New roads to travel. It is wonderful to take off and just meander: find a new road and be surprised to discover another hamlet, farm, wildlife and, with a bit of luck, a pub!

It's all good fun and tests our state of "togetherness". If two people can survive motoring holidays, they deserve a medal!

CARRY ON MOTORING!

FOOD FOR THOUGHT

On the last night of our holiday in the Chianti region of Tuscany, we decided to eat out. The Italian owners of the farmhouse where we were staying, recommended a local restaurant. They kindly phoned ahead and reserved a table for us.

With a hand to the mouth kissing gesture they assured us that the food was *MMMMMMMAM ... Magnifico*, and it would only take us twenty minutes to get there.

Simple, we thought, just follow their instructions. Turn left at the bottom of the road, past the large farmhouse owned by the family Puccini, no relation to the maestro although there were rumours.

Continue on that road for two kilometres then turn right. NO ... left. Our hosts spoke to us in English, but argued in Italian. Eventually with a great deal of discussion and *Mama Mia*'s from the *Signora* ... they agreed.

Turn right at the fork in the road, continue for about one kilometre. Then, just as the road bends, take the path beside the three large cypress tress. Fine. Which three? Considering that Tuscany has more cypress trees than anywhere I know.

We smiled and agreed to drive on the road. Where else? We jumped into our little car and took off. It was a balmy evening and the fire had just gone out of the sun. Seconds later and it was dark, very dark.

We followed the road down through the hills, down and down in a spiral, negotiating a few hairpin bends with great care. In the distance, car headlights snaked across the inky black countryside like gigantic glow worms.

I looked at the car clock. It was three quarters of an hour since we had left the farmhouse. Twenty minutes Italian time is obviously different from twenty minutes British time.

It may be the fact that Italians drive like bats out of hell, or should I say Dante's Inferno. Certainly it has to be said that our Fiat Panda has its limitations.

The road was now little more than a dirt track, a metal road. They call it, and it certainly felt like one. We finally reached the floor of the valley. The road stretched out ahead, we presumed.

We were the only car on that particular road, *somewhere* in the heart of Tuscany.

How romantic. Are you kidding? There had been no signs of human life for the last hour.

No lights. No farmhouses. I kept quiet, afraid to state the obvious.

I could only just see the outline of the hills on either side of us. I cursed the rustic simplicity of it all, surely a few lights wouldn't spoil it.

What if we break down? We can't risk leaving the car. Too much wildlife around us. Snakes, wildcats, boar. OH GREAT ... I'm trying hard to think of a wonderful meal. AND NOT TO PANIC.

Suddenly from out of nowhere a loud blast of a horn and something low, expensive and Italian shot past us. It would be an understatement to say that my husband uttered a few impolite words.

He ranted and raved that it must be some bloody Romeo rushing to meet someone else's wife for a bit of the other.

I wondered what it would be like to have a Latin Lover who drove his red shiny sports car through the navy blue night just to see me. I'm sure his car was red, probably a Ferrari or a Maserati. I sighed.

"Why are you sighing?" my better half snapped.

"Eh. I think we are lost, maybe we should just go back." I faltered.

Well, I thought, sometimes this happens when we travel a fair distance for a good meal but this is becoming ridiculous. We are lost.

I know you are ravenous darling, and you are *not* very nice to know at the moment.

I suspect that your personality change goes back to the time when man was the hunter and had to kill his meat. I am hungry too.

At last, could this be the place? In front of us I can just make out the shape of a long low farmhouse or is it a mirage? No. that, is the desert. Might as well be, lack of food is having its effect.

As we drew near we could see lights among the trees. We drove into a little courtyard. This must be it. Five cars were parked there.

No *ristorante* sign, but his quite common, if it is a place known only to the locals.

Four horrific looking dogs, the size of small ponies, were sniffing about. I exaggerate, but they were, big, black and mean. I was terrified and refused to get out of the car.

An elderly woman appeared and let forth a torrent of Italian. The dogs stood their ground snarling and barking.

She advanced on them, her voice louder than ever. She won ... the dogs backed off.

We got out of the car to be greeted by the little round woman. She spoke to us in quick fire Italian. We had no idea what she said.

I struggled. "*Mangiare* ... reservation ... *mangiare* eight o'clock ... sorry we are late." I pointed to my watch.

My better half tried. "*Mangiare.*" She silenced him with a wave of the hand and a fierce look. She motioned to us then pointed to the ground. She disappeared inside.

"I don't know what she said. Do you think that she means us to wait here?"

The woman came out with the man of the house. He glared at us and rattled off about 100 words a minute.

I stuttered, "*Non capisco* ... only ... *un poco.*"

"*Deutche?*" he interrupted.

"NO ... Scottish ... *la Gran Bretagna.*"

"AHHH ... Whisky ... Princess Diana." He smiled least I think the change of expression was a smile.

I smiled and ventured "Do you speak English?" He shook his head and turned to his wife. She scowled and beckoned for us to go inside. She escorted us to a table at the back of the room. Her husband came back with a basket of bread.

He poured wine for us from a bottle with a very wet label, then he stomped off.

My husband sipped a little wine. "MMMmm it's good." He lifted the bottle to look at the label. It came off and stuck to his hand.

I laughed, "A very good year ... more like a month."

I looked around the dimly lit room. It was small, just like someone's living room. Plaques depicting scenes from Italian country life covered the walls. We occupied one table, there was a vacant one, and sitting at a long table were ten or twelve men.

I leaned across the table. "James I think it is the Last Supper, there's twelve of them."

Elizabeth ... you and your imagination."

Now the man of the house was talking to the man at the head of the table. They were both looking in our direction. "James, they're talking about us, they keep looking over."

The man of the house ambled over to our table. He pointed to the men, then us, then to his mouth, muttered, "*mangiare*" and walked off.

"I think he means we eat the same as they do."

"I think so, but whatever it is I wish that they would hurry up." moaned James.

"So do I ... It's a bit odd, all these men are wearing business suits. I suppose ... secret deals."

I studied the men. All of them reeked of money. All Italian, all good looking, well groomed, wearing suits that proclaimed designer labels.

The man at the head of the table was quite striking, about forty-five, chiselled features almost cruel looking. His dark wavy hair was brushed straight back. There was no doubt, he was in charge.

The woman served them soup from a large cauldron which her husband carried to the table. We were then served the same soup and more bread. Ten minutes later, large plates of pasta were put down before us.

The woman stood by and opened a bottle of red wine. When James protested, the woman pointed over to the man at the head of the table, he smiled and nodded.

James studied the bottle of wine, it was the best in the area. "We'll have to drink it and thank him later." I babbled on as we ate our way though meat done in herbs and wild mushrooms, two cheeses and coffee.

As we helped ourselves to more coffee, the man at the head of the table came across to us. In almost perfect English he said, "I am always pleased to welcome guests." He shook hands with James. He took my hand and kissed it, his dark eyes making contact with mine as he did so.

"I hope you enjoy your food and wine, it is on the house." He flashed a gold filling smile in my direction. James protested. "It is done." the man shrugged and spread his hands outwards. "Now please you have a grappa."

"Thank you , but not for me," I said hastily.

"For you *Signora*, something more delicate, made from rose petals. When you are ready to leave you will follow my driver. He will escort you to the farmhouse. You will not get lost again."

He smiled arrogantly and returned to his table.

James sipped his grappa. I sipped my rose liqueur. "This is lovely ... I was thinking ... ehm tomorrow we could ..."

"Finish it and let's get out of here."

A thick set little man in a chauffeur's uniform appeared, we followed him outside and got in to our car. He opened the door of a huge black limo and got inside. He flashed his lights at us and we followed him.

"James ... JAMES. I'M SCARED. Do you think we should be following him?"

"We have no option."

"But we might be robbed or ... anything."

"Don't be silly, we are not worth robbing."

"But ... these men ... they were a bit menacing and the one who spoke to us ... he ..."

James tutted in annoyance. I continued in silent thought. The man who spoke to us was used to getting his own way. He was a species who was very dangerous and highly attractive to women.

We continued to follow the shiny black car, its powerful headlights illuminating the road like searchlights.

"It's as well we are not at home, you're well over the limit ... What if the police?"

"What police?"

Suddenly the car flashed its lights at us and disappeared. We sat there. It took about five minutes before we realised where we were.

We were at the foot of the road leading to the farmhouse. How did they know? We chugged up the hill and stopped outside the door. All the lights were on and the dogs were setting up a barking contest.

Our landlord came running out, "You are alright? You are alright? We so worried. You very late."

The *Signora* grabbed James by the arm, "you are alright?"

"Yes."

"Come in, sit down, have a grappa."

We told them what we had eaten, about the men and our escort.

"Maria, she look after you good?" queried the *Signora*.

"Oh yes." I said.

"You tell Maria I send you?"

"We-ell, she didn't seem to understand her husband."

"Husband, Maria no have husband. The men?"

I broke in, "Yes, twelve of them, I heard one of them call the man in charge, *Signor Franconi.*"

"AHHHH ... *Mama Mia* ... *Mama Mia* ... *Franconi* she spat out his name .. He is back again .. AHHHHH"

Her husband put his arm around her and said, "Long time ago ... no worry ... *Buona notte.*"

We tottered upstairs, tomorrow we would go home. "James, do you think we were in the wrong place? The *Signora* ... do you think she meant ... these men .. THE FAMILY?"

James replied with a chorus of ZZZZZZZZZZZZ.

IMAGINE ALL THE PEOPLE

It is August, a day of oppressive heat and sulky sky and I am in Pompeii. To most people this means a city situated on the south east slope of Mt. Vesuvius and dramatically obliterated by the volcano. It is easy to imagine way back to another August, the one in AD79, probably a day like today, when the giant tummy of the mountain rumbled and spewed out its deadly contents.

There had been a warning a few days before. Loud roaring noises, gurglings and tremors from deep within the earth. Houses shaken, walls split. Animals had become restless and birds flew back and forth in a nervous frenzy.

Some of the people had become afraid and fled, many of them remembering the horrific effects of the earthquake of AD62. Others remained, thinking that it could not possibly happen again.

I look around me, modern times, modern people of the tourist tribes, tramping on the graves of the ancients. I can almost feel the unseen eyes of tormented spirits watching me. If only they could speak. I sit down on part of a wall bearing ancient graffiti. Confessions of undying passion, political slogans and honesty of shopkeepers. What's new?

The sun is blinking from behind the clouds. Whew, it's hot. Hot as Dante's Inferno. I take a few sips from my large bottle of water. I wonder if the ladies of Pompeii ever sat in the sun. They did visit the baths or *The Thermae* as they were known.

This is where men often conducted business and the women, in a separate section caught up with the gossip.

Then, what did the ladies do?

Possibly did what all women do, they went shopping. I can see them browsing at the open fronted shops, drooling over the gold jewellery and buying expensive cloth. They would leave the mundane shopping for food to their servants.

I drink some more water and consult my guide book. It suggests reading the vivid account by Pliny the younger, who saw the ashes and pumice stone shoot into the air and fall on the decks of the ships of the fleet anchored at Misenum.

Pompeii was covered over with a layer of lapilli and ashes spread to a height of twenty three feet, weighing heavily on the roofs of houses, breaking and crushing them.

After the eruption, torrents of rain and wind diluted the lava and ashes into a slimy magma which slid into the streets solidifying buildings and everything else in its path.

People who died became casts of disintegrating corpses. The shape of which has been preserved by the liquid lava which hardened round the bodies where they fell. Most of the casts can be seen in the museum in Naples. Burning mud poured from the gaping mouth of the mountain and poured down the slopes. When it reached the sea, the waves boiled and sizzled and came together in a mighty struggle.

Galleons and merchant ships were crushed and showers of lapilli, ash, flint and stones crashed down on the scorched villas and farms. The people could not see in the darkness caused by the smoke. The fumes from the gasses stifled their breathing and many fell down dead.

Herculaneum, further to the south west and, towns fifteen miles away suffered the same fate as Pompeii and disappeared under layers of excessively hard mineral masses. Even as far away as Sorrento, there were reports of burning cinders falling on the town.

I touch the wall beside me and marvel that it has been here all the time. Imagine the panic. Imagine all the people.

No wonder they were afraid and thought that the Gods were angry with them and that Jupiter and Neptune were fighting a duel.

Ohhh ... this sultry heat, I could do with a shower of rain.

To think that all that time ago, they could cope with heavy rain and flooding here. High pavements and large round stepping stones in the middle of the streets. Well, some of the streets, the others were for horses and chariots, you can still see the ruts in the road.

What a place this must have been. It was a holiday resort for very rich Romans, who had large villas with pictures painted on the walls, like a sort of private art gallery.

It was a city for the sophisticated populous and the peasantry. It was wealthy and self sufficient. They traded luxury goods with overseas countries while still under the patronage of Rome.

The people worked hard and played hard. They loved the bloodthirsty goings on at the amphitheatre. Gladiators fighting each other often to the death, or fighting animals and killing them. Gladiators were the pop stars of ancient times and enjoyed many favours from the ladies of all ranks.

The oldest profession in the world was legal and special Houses of Assignation seemed to be situated in almost every street. They were easy to find as they were represented on the paving stones outside by exaggerated carvings of male manhood.

Life was for living to the full, and is still part of Italian philosophy today.

Too soon it is time for me to leave. I wish I could stay here alone and go back in time, on my terms of course.

The sky is turning a menacing black and blue. A distant rumble of thunder quickly becomes crashing cymbals of a decibel level that makes the ground tremble.

Fork lightning zigzags into the crater of Vesuvius. To think that only one hour ago, I was sitting on the edge looking down into the mouth of the volcano. More ear splitting thunder, more silent silver lightning.

I stop and stare. The Gods must be angry, but what a show they are putting on, absolutely magnificent. The rain is pounding down in staccato time. I am soaked through, but I don't care.

A GOOD DAY

She stood at the bus stop feeling sorry for herself. If only she had learned to drive, but James had always been there to take her wherever she wanted to go.

She sighed, "Aye, you looked after me so well. Oh James. I miss you so much." She shifted her feet becoming annoyed at the bitter wind that was finding its way through her warm clothes.

That daughter of ours asks me down for a coffee, then tells me that her car is at the garage for an MOT. Next thing, she suggests that since I have recently got a bus pass, why don't I use it? Hmmm.

"Where is the bus?" she muttered as she looked along the street. "Oh here it comes, at last."

The small bus drew to a halt, the doors swished open and the step sank to pavement level.

As she stepped aboard the driver greeted her, "Morning hen, Where to?"

"Umm. Gourock ... Cloch Road."

"Right. I hope you've got the right money, no change you know what I mean?"

She held out her bus pass.

"A bus pass? You're kiddin' me?" He smiled at her and his blue eyes twinkled.

"Umm. No ... thank you." she snatched the bus pass away from him stumbled halfway up the bus and sat down. She adjusted her bag on her lap and almost at the same moment someone tapped her on the shoulder. She looked round.

"I thought it was you, Aileen Black, isn't it?"

"Yes, and umm ... Maureen?"

"That's me. How are you? My father told me that James had died six months ago. Heart attack he said."

"Yes. Quite a shock. Just got to get on with it. And you?"

"I am divorced. I'm home now for a holiday and to try and persuade my father to come back to Florida with me to live. He loves it there."

"That would be good. What are you doing on the bus?"

"It's easier and I don't want to drive over here. Too fast for me. What about you?"

"Oh I never learned to drive. James decided that he alone would drive and that was it. Women drivers no way."

"I know. Mind you, the bus, it's not the same. Remember the clippies with their hats pulled down to eye level and held in place by two kirby grips?"

"All that time away and you haven't forgotten and what about the ticket machine at knee level and the shouts of "Come oan get aff.""

They both burst out laughing. How could you get on and off at the same time?

"Aye, there were a few nippie sweeties among them, although some of the men from the yards thought it best to refer to them as cheerful cookies."

"Oh Maureen that's going back a bit."

They started to laugh again when the driver interrupted.

"Right girls back there one of you was getting off at the library remember?"

"Oh it's me." Maureen stood up quickly and shouted to the driver "Hang on a minute, I must give Aileen my phone number." She scribbled on a small piece of paper and gave it to Aileen.

"Phone me. I mean it. I've enjoyed the chat. Phone me tonight about six. Bye."

Aileen waved to her as she got off the bus.

A few more people got on board and off they went. The bus picked its way through Gourock and along past the outdoor pool.

Aileen got up and made her way to the door. The driver stopped and nodded to her. "Well that was a good blether. You haven't been on a bus for years hen have you? Bye hen. See you later."

Jennifer was at the door to meet her mother. "Hi Mum, cone on in, sit down. Well going on the bus wasn't that bad, was it? Let's have coffee first then you can tell me. No ... I can't wait to tell you something. I'm ... you are going to be a granny."

"What? Really? Oh Jen. I can't believe it. What about Peter? He'll be so excited." She jumped up and hugged her daughter. They cried. They laughed. They talked.

Later that night when Aileen was tucked up in bed, she thought about the events of the day. She had done it. She had gone on the bus. The driver was chatty and nice. She had met an old friend and she had phoned her and they were going to meet.

She smiled, but the most important thing was that she was going to be a Granny. Oh if only James was here to share the wonderful news.

She would still think about him and miss him, but there would be a new baby to look after.

She closed her eyes. Today had been a good day.

19

BITTERSWEET

I suddenly feel like a piece of thistledown that is being blown about in the wind. My heart is leaping about in my chest and my stomach seems to be full of fluttering butterflies. I gulp air and let it out again in a sigh.

"What's wrong, are you feeling ill?" Richard pats my hand.

"No, it's just ..."

Celia Davenport butts in "It's the jet lag, but you are OK?"

I can only apologise, we thought you were arriving yesterday.

"That's OK. Thank you for the flowers and the invitation. It's nice to see you both again, last time we met it was Paris wasn't it?"

"Yes, Ah Paris. They say it's better to have loved and lost in Paris, than never to have loved at all, if only. she chuckled.

"What are you saying Pumpkin?" Matthew asks, winking at me.

"I'm just saying tonight's concert is a romantic programme. Thought I'd remind you of how it used to be."

I can feel myself go hot and cold. What a shock ... How it used to be ... the programme.

A Salute to Maxwell Louis Olivier De Vere on his 45th Birthday … and a photograph.

I can't believe it. I've managed to avoid him all these years. I knew that he had gone to the States, but last I heard he lived in the lap of luxury in Palm Beach, and didn't do any touring.

Oh God. I sigh. Richard squeezes my hand.

"I know. Are you alright?"

"Yes, I'll manage, but I'll need a stiff drink at the interval." I glance at him. He is still a good looking man, a bit rotund now. His silver hair is immaculate. He still has a twinkle in his denim blue eyes, and he still knows what to do about it.

Oh Richard, you are my anchor. I am so lucky to have you. I'm glad I make you happy. You deserve it. You are such a good man. You understood. You married me.

The lights dim, and the wistful sound of violins drifts round Carnegie Hall. I focus on the orchestra. Abstract shapes, gleaming brass, the red brown polished wood of the strings, negative spaces that are men and women in black.

My thoughts return to the past. Paris … I was only eighteen when I met you Maxwell, and you were twenty-five.

I was doing a year's study in the French language. And you, Aunt Liz, you were supposed to keep me out of trouble, that's why I was sent to stay with you.

What did you do? You took me to a reception at the Embassy, and there was Maxwell, playing Chopin.

We were introduced. We smiled at each other, and from that first moment, we both knew. It was love.

As I stood looking up into your dark brooding eyes, the world seemed to spin round and round, and explode in tiny stars. My body tingled from head to foot. I felt as if I had been switched on to all the power on earth.

You phoned me later that evening and told me it was a

coup de foudre, did I know the phrase. I said no, and you explained it to me. Love at first sight.

Oh yes, it certainly was. All the clichés were true. I was bowled over. It was April, and Paris was bursting out of her winter chrysalis. The chestnuts would soon be in bloom.

There was a certain feeling in the air, a quiver of anticipation. Outdoor cafe life had begun again. Men and women appraised each other en passant. Romance lingered all around us.

We both liked the same things, the same music, the same books, art, food, wine. And the little hotel on the Left Bank, and our little room with the faded blue and white wallpaper, and the big bed where we first made love.

I loved Paris. The smell of freshly baked bread in the morning, the artists, the writers, the students playing chess. I loved it.

"Interval, follow me." commanded Celia, jolting me back to reality. Richard took my hand as we followed the Davenports through the crowd.

"In here. If we are lucky, Maxwell De Vere will honour us with his presence. It depends on how he is feeling. If he comes we will make a lot of money."

"Well off you go Pumpkin. Paula and Steve are waving to you. I'll look after Victoria and Richard."

"You don't mind, do you? I'll be back in a moment."

Matthew shook his head, "I hate all this hobnobbing, even if it is for charity. Celia is such a snob. We are old money, but that doesn't mean we own the world."

He laughed, "It does mean that we can buy more antiques from you, before you decide to retire. I can recommend retirement you know."

"I'm sure you can." Richard countered.

"It's a daughter you have, isn't it? Do you think that she might take over the business?"

"No. Never, she is not interested."

"Is she married?"

"No. She has plenty of time, she is only twenty, besides I can't afford it." Richard grinned.

Oh No. No. No. Here comes Celia and two of her friends ... and Maxwell. The tall woman, all teeth and bouffant hair introduces me to Maxwell Louis Olivier De Vere.

I look up. He bows low, takes my hand and kisses it. His dark brooding eyes meet mine. Look. Register. Then cloud again. "Madame." He steps back and shakes hands with Richard, then moves away.

I am trembling, and I know my face has flushed. He doesn't recognise me. He doesn't know me. Well I suppose it's a long time ago. And I have changed from long blonde hair to a short bog, and lighter blonde. I'm still slim.

He is doing the rounds on the other side of the room. I can't stop looking at him. He is still handsome. His hair is still dark with just a hint of grey at the temples.

His eyes look sad and a bit sunken. His mouth. Oh Maxwell. I raise my champagne glass to my lips and traces of his after shave linger on my hand, Maxwell.

Suddenly he looks directly at me. I can see recognition. He is moving. He is coming over. Oh No. I edge round and turn my back to him. It's no use. The dark brown velvet voice still sends messages to my spine. "Madame."

I turn to him just as Celia's well rounded figure decides to bustle between us. She grabs his arm and looks up into his face, batting her eyelashes for all she is worth. He stares at me over her head. I stare back.

Celia calls over to Matthew, who ignores here. Richard leaves our little group to get another drink. I excuse myself to go to the rest room.

As I reach the door, Maxwell is beside me. "Madame." Someone calls to him, "Maxwell, fifteen minutes.

"Yes." He turns to me, "Madame, do you like Chopin?"

"Yes" I whisper.

His face lights up and he smiles, that familiar heart wrenching smile.

"And ... is it you? Victoria?"

I nod, not trusting myself to speak.

"Maxwell, you have ten minutes."

I move away and he is gone.

"Well Victoria, what was Maxwell saying to you. Celia questioned as we returned to our seats.

"Oh nothing much. Was I enjoying the concert?"

"He is a dream, isn't he? Quite a ladies man."

"Is he married?" I ask.

"He was, but she left him after a year, said he was married to his music. According to Paula, you met her, he had to marry to please his mother. She threatened to cut off his allowance if he didn't. She even chose the bride."

Being French, he was supposed to carry on the family business the vineyards. If his father had been alive there would have been no problem. He was English, you know. Killed in the war, his mother, was another story."

"Maxwell wanted to be a concert pianist. His mother relented. She realised that she had already spoiled his life. He took off round the world on tour and always the women."

"Did he ever re-marry? Have children?"

"No. None of the women meant anything to him. Now he's dying. Cancer. This is the reason for tonight's concert. He wanted to help the fundraising."

That's why the reception was held at the interval. He is so ill, he will have to go home immediately after he plays."

The conductor taps his baton and announces. "Monsieur De Vere."

Maxwell walks on to the stage, holds up his hands to quell the applause and says "Ladies and Gentlemen, tonight I shall play for the last time. I am going away. I am retiring." he laughs. "and I am so young."

The audience begin to applaud again, but he carries on speaking, "Please, this is a very special evening. It is my Birthday. Tonight, I dedicate to my youth, a very special lady, and to Chopin."

"His music can be likened to a love affair, a Grand Passion, that happens only once in a ... lifetime, and is never forgotten. I shall play four pieces, firstly:-

THE PRELUDE – an introduction, that first tentative advance.

ETUDE – an exercise, a study, an interpretation.

is it love?

VALSE BRILLIANTE – Yes. Yes. that feeling of happiness sparkling and bubbling like champagne.

When lovers live on pink clouds, high above the universe and finally, the hauntingly beautiful

NOCTURNE – The night music of remembrance and despair when fate deals lovers a cruel blow.

I hope that you will all enjoy my presentation of this passionate and brilliant music of starlight and romance.

I can feel the tears in my eyes, Oh Maxwell. Maxwell, I never stopped loving you. You remembered our pink cloud and our Valse Brilliante.

When you went to see your mother to tell her about us, and you didn't come back ... and your wedding plans became public. What was I to think? I didn't know.

Oh Maxwell, it seemed so simple just to tell your mother about us. I couldn't understand why you didn't contact me.

It wasn't till years later that I found out what kind of person your mother was. My Aunt Liz wrote to me from Paris. She had a boyfriend in the wine trade who knew the whole story.

Your mother had taken to bed with a supposed heart

attack when you told her that you wanted to marry me. Her tantrums, her selfishness. You had to live with her behaviour all her life.

Her snobbery and obsession with the family name, her insistence that you marry within your own circle and nationality or she would cut off your allowance.

You did as she asked, put honour before love. Too late when you found out her guilty secret. Too late for us. Too late. She had ruined your life.

Your mother was illegitimate but had been brought up as a child of the count at the chateau. She was terrified anyone would find out and she would be disgraced.

Your wife's mother and father knew, but their silence was guaranteed by striking a bargain to unite the two vineyards by your marriage.

I was sent back home to London, and Richard. He was a family friend and a frequent visitor to our house. He had always listened to my woes.

Poor man, his life had been sad. He was only married for seven years, when his wife and baby daughter were killed in a car crash. And they had waited all that time for a child.

The tears are streaming down my face ... Richard hands me a handkerchief and murmurs, "It's time, you have to do it now. You owe it to both of them."

I nod. I know, but he has not time. I sniff. Maxwell, I stare at him through my tears. He looks intense, Ill, but he is playing brilliantly, weaving the music into moody ribbons of passion and pathos.

Celia is sniffing, women all around me are sniffing trying to control their tears.

Oh Maxwell, there must be time for you to meet your daughter.

JUST DESSERTS

I have a dream. I am lost in a paradise where temptation comes in many forms, my favourite being, good looking, rich and dark. Nothing is forbidden, and I make no attempt to resist what is on offer to me. I cannot, because I am weak, and give in easily to my baser instincts.

I am wandering through a garden of brown, dark brown and white. There is a strange smell of chocolate in the air. Chocolate? I touch a white flower, it is smooth as satin. I sniff it. I break off a petal. I taste it. It *is* chocolate.

I run to a tree. A leaf falls to the ground. I pick it up. More chocolate, I pick up a rose, and pluck its velvet black petals. I bite into its oozing soft centre.

Suddenly chocolate soldiers are marching towards me. One of them comes alive. He speaks to me.

"Stop dreaming, it's time to go, don't you want any dinner?"

It is our Anniversary, and here we are sitting in this rather posh restaurant. A quiet dinner for two, or dinner *a deux*, as they say in this establishment.

Picture it, soft pink tablecloth, flickering candlelight,

gleaming silver, sparkling crystal. The scent of flowers, if only the freesia didn't remind me of funerals.

Pleasant conversation, that's a joke, when food is on offer most men don't want to talk AND eat. It is always easy to tell who the married couples are, they never talk whilst having dinner. The singles do, they are still too busy making an impression on each other.

It can be amusing to watch men go through the palaver of wine tasting. They look grim and serious, as they try to convince everyone that they know all about it.

Go on, get the nose in, have a good sniff. Tastes of plums, with a hint of pineapple and every other fruit in the world. What happened to the grape? Jilly Cooper surely can't be wrong.

The truth is that after the aperitif, and the ritual choosing from the menu, most men are starving, and all they want is food. They go through the motions, but they really don't care, whether the rosy glow from the candles is romantic or not.

Women, especially those of indeterminate age, are thankful for the dim light. It hides blemishes and wrinkles, sorry laughter lines.

Going out for dinner is an event which I enjoy, even when it is to celebrate an umpteenth anniversary. I love food. I am a foodie or food freak. I seem to drink wine at a faster pace than my other half, which results in a nod and a glare. One must savour it you know, not gulp it down like coke.

At last, the first course arrives. Consommé, with sherry. I do like it, honestly, it's not just an excuse for another drink. I'll skip the fish course. I always get a bone, even if there isn't any.

The main course, yes, steak, well done, with or without E. Colli or B.S.E. yes, with the whisky sauce, that may kill all known germs. Just a few chips. Must watch the cholesterol level.

Cheeseboard? Why not? A dodda the mouldy one please, and two oatcakes. Now, for something I've patiently waited for all evening. My favourite course, and when I realise that I am a glutton, and gluttony is a sin. I am guilty, but I cannot help it. I am at the mercy of a raging sweet tooth, and there is no cure.

I blame it all on Mary Queen of Scots. She brought her court to Edinburgh. All those French chefs and pastry makers are responsible for dour Scots actually enjoying something.

Here it comes, a trundling wooden feast of delight. The sweet trolley. I ignore Harrison Ford or was it Jeremy Paxman tonight, no it is my old man, anyway I ignore him in favour of the waiter who is rhyming off the list of goodies.

I could listen to the French accent all evening, he sounds just like Sacha Distel. I wonder if he can sing like him. I listen and translate the items into my own thoughts.

Banoffi Pie, yes that's the creamy banana concoction.

Chocolate Eclairs ... slim elegant sophisticated.

Atholl Brose ... alcoholic porridge oats and cream.

Black Forest gateau ... oodles of black cherries soaked in Kirsch and cream ... thoughts of athletic blond Germans in leather shorts, yodelling like mad.

Rum Babas ... Desert Island, and swaying palms in the moonlight.

Crème Brûlée ... French egg custard.

Scotch Trifle ... full of sherry and goo.

And ... Chocolate Cake ... Good looking, rich, dark and chocolatey ... Food of the Gods ... Temptation at the highest level ... The Ultimate Aphrodisiac ...

What to choose. Yes, it is possible to have chocolate cake,

and, some of that. The waiter answers snootily. With cream or ice cream. Both ... He looks at me in disgust.

I feel like asking him if he has heard of Rab Ha, the Glasgow Glutton. I think I may be his female equivalent. Yes. My eyes are bigger than my bel ... stomach.

Coffee and tablet, why not? Liqueur? I'm tempted, Better not. I'll just have another piece of tablet. Now it's time to drive home. This seat belt is far too tight, or could it be the waistband on my skirt that is cutting me in half.

Did this road have all these bends on the way down. It's making me dizzy. Oh Oh. I think I'm about to suffer death by chocolate, ice cream and everything else.

"STOP THE CAR ... I'M GOING TO BE SICK."

OBSERVATIONS

I take a few faltering steps nearer the edge. I inch forward a little, my toes are over in free space. I look down at the rails and they swim up to meet me. Go on then. I'm shaking and cold, like some exotic cocktail, its spirit weakened by too many ice cubes. My inner voice screams at me. NO ... NO ... NO ... Don't be so stupid. I can hear the train. I try to move, but my legs are encased in concrete.

People are running along the platform. The train rattles in and hurtles to a halt disgorging its passengers. I am jostled and pushed aboard. The doors slide together with a hiss. I sit down I am weightless, my body has left me.

"Are ye awright hen?" asks a plump little woman beside me. I nod. "Well ye don't look it. Yur that white. Hiv ye got a right dose o'the flu? Get away hame, make a big toddy an' get tae yer bed. I shake my head. "Oh it's no a man is it? Nane o' them worth it. A big toddy hen." She pats my shoulder as she stands up to get off at the next stop.

Oh no. I'm going to cry again. Oh no ... oh no. I can't. I musn't. Advice from a concerned stranger. Concerned, that's more than my husband was last night. "Judith," he said.

"There is no easy way to say this. I've met someone else, it's as simple as that."

I still can't take it in. I'm being tossed over like a salad. Me. Judith Benson, aged twenty eight, dark, slim, passable in the looks stakes. ME ... DIVORCE.

The clitter clatter of the Orange seems to mock me. Divorce divorce ... DIVORCE. It's me. It's me. It's happening to ME. I'm going to be the other half of the one in four couples who divorce.

I wish my stomach wouldn't rumble so loudly. I suppose I must be hungry. I was so sick last night. My head is so woozy. I need a cup of tea.

Oh no. A whiff of curry on someone's breath wafts perilously close. Oh NO. I must not be sick. My stomach threatens to disagree. I can't believe it. Divorce ... Oh Alan. It's all fallen apart, like an egg that I have carefully lifted from the fridge and tried hard not to drop, but I end up unintentionally squashing it in my hand.

Did I do that to our marriage? NO, we both did. I suppose that the cracks were always there, from the very beginning. We didn't really have a lot in common. It was lust at first sight, opposites attract, we married a month after we met, and that was only two years ago.

Yes Alan, you met her one the first day you went to the London office nearly six months ago. You had to socialise. There she was and it just happened ...

When Alan? Five weeks after you met her. You waited that long? You, all six feet of you, with your brown eyes and that lock of dark hair that won't stay in place.

The Orange shoogles round a corner, I slide forward. A young student opposite stares into space, nodding his head, personal stereo his conversation. Without looking up to check where she is, the girl next to him, closes her book, and as if programmed gets off at the next stop.

An older woman clutching a large shiny carrier bag sits down beside me, she smiles and pats the bag "I've got my outfit for my son's wedding." She prattles on wedding ... hmmm. I don't care Ohh it's not her fault. I listen and I think I smile. She sees a friend and moves up the carriage to tell her the good news.

I should get off this train. I'm looking the loop again. Should I sell the flat? No. I like this area, Byres Road. I'll need a lawyer I can afford a good one, just as well my marketing job pays well.

And you Alan, you won't starve, with your job as a broker, her good salary and her rich daddy. You'll never be too tired for her. How did we end up like this. I wish we had never met at that party No that is not true. The first year was wonderful, till work and ambition took over.

No time to talk to each other, passing by in the morning, going to bed at night, too tired to make love. I don't suppose you think about what you are putting me through. I don't suppose you care you've turned my life upside down. I have to face our friends, their pity, for some, their triumph. I have to pick up the pieces in public. I call him all the nasty things I can think of and that includes words I didn't realise I knew. I am a modern woman is this the price I have to pay for equality?

A hand on my arm, "Is the next stop suitable for the Western infirmary?" asks the elderly lady sitting beside me.

"Umm ... yes, but it is a bit of a walk."

"Oh that's alright dear, it can't be as far as the last time when I got off at Hillhead and had to walk down Byres Road. It's the stop before that isn't it?"

"Yes, but I'm not sure what the visiting hours are."

"I ... I'm not visiting, I ... I ... ehm ... I'm going for the results of tests."

"I'm sure everything will be alright."

"I hope so." her voice wavers, "I just wish it was all over."

"Is anyone coming to meet you?"

"No dear, none of the family know. I couldn't trouble them, and my friends, well it's something I'd rather do myself, although right now ... I wish." Her hands are shaking as she fiddles with her handbag. I hear myself say, "This is the stop. I'll walk with you." As we walk along Dumbarton Road, she is telling me her life story. When we reach the entrance to the hospital, she looks at me, I smile as we go inside together.

What am I doing here? I don't know this elderly lady, but today she needs someone and it's me. Alan doesn't need me. At this moment my only true love is the greatest city I know. So don't cry for me Glasgow. I'm not leaving you. I'll survive, after all people make Glasgow.

The nurse calls out another name, the elderly lady stand up. "That's me dear. Thank you for staying with me. Good-bye."

"I'm not going anywhere. I'll be here when you come out."

"Thank you dear." She smiles and I can see tears in her eyes.

NEPTUNE AND THE MERMAID

Anthony had always loved the sea. In fact water of any kind. When we first met, he tried to convince me that he remembered the feeling of the water, when he was a baby in his bath.

He even had a photograph to prove it, the one I'm looking at now, of a happy gurgling infant with a shock of black hair and dark eyes. The beginning of a life that never reached the allotted span.

I shuffle the rest of the photographs. I can feel myself start to smile. One of us together , so young, so in love, me with my left bank look, all kohl and mascara eyes peeping out from under a fringe of long dark hair.

I can feel the tears. NO. NO. No more that is enough for today. I must not cry. I cross the room to the window and look out at the river.

It is a beautiful day. The sky is bright blue. The hills glow emerald and ochre. The sun is sparkling on the water like lots of tiny diamonds. Almost Mediterranean, but not quite.

I can hardly believe that I am looking at the Clyde and across to the Cowal hills. My artist's eye automatically deciding how to paint the scene. I sigh, funny how the senses are sharpened by sadness and grief.

Stop it. Stop it Elizabeth. I tell myself. Anthony always said, "Here today, gone tomorrow, life's too short for all that sorrow." I suppose so, but ... I sniff to stop the tears.

I sit down by the window with my sketch pad and pencils. Remember Anthony, we couldn't agree on the best way to use this room. In the end we decided that we could both use it, as a perfect studio cum study, cum den.

Gosh, eighteen years ago, just seems like yesterday since we met. You had been at the Boat Club, gone out rowing, larked about and had fallen in, you and my brother. He brought you home for a change of clothes.

There you were, all six foot two of you, dark hair plastered to your head, telling me that you were Neptune, King of the Sea, and I was a mermaid that you had come to rescue.

The sea was your life, wasn't it Darling? I can hear your voice, full of excitement, telling me, "I'm a student at the Watt College. Next year I'm going to sea."

You rumbled on, "My great Grandfather and my Grandfather both went to sea. I want to carry on the family tradition. It's a man's life you know. It's a challenge ... man against nature."

"It's Nelson, Raleigh, Hornblower ... It's It's part of me. You're my little mermaid, my Lorelei, my siren, luring me on to the rocks ... to have your wicked way with me."

I hear myself reply, "But surely if I'm a mermaid luring you, then it's to destroy you."

"Well, I suppose so ... that's a thing, when I die I want to be buried the Viking way, you know truss me up in a long boat. Set me on fire. Push me out to sea and with any luck I'll reach Valhalla."

Now the dusk is turning the hills to a deep pink against a backdrop of red sky. I finish my sketches and go to bed.

I wake again in the middle of the night and sit bolt upright. I'm sweating. My heart is thumping and bumping around my chest. I'm gasping for breath.

It's the same tortuous dream. Will it never end? I'm walking on the Esplanade. It is so cold. There is a curtain of white mist floating and twisting upwards from the river. A white boat glides through it.

Suddenly there is a loud explosion and orange flames shoot into the air and drip down blood red over the frozen water. A rainbow of sparks spew out and there is the smell of turpentine.

Anthony materialises from the flames. He stares at me, least the black sockets where his eyes should be, stare at me. The dark slash that is his mouth opens and closes like a fish.

Oh I can't sleep. I get up and totter downstairs. A brandy might help. I go to the cabinet and pour myself a large one, and carry it to the den.

Oh Anthony ... I do miss you so. You were a handsome man. I remember being so proud of you when you came home on leave for the first time.

You were wearing your merchant navy uniform and your camel duffle. This coat was a stamp of approval worn by nice decent boys, the kind to take home to mother.

I loved showing you off to my friends when we went to a coffee bar or the Saturday night hop at the Boat Club. I learned about trad jazz and a few other things.

They were innocent times, when nice girls didn't and nice boys didn't ask. However there was always an exception to the rule. Wasn't there Anthony?

It was so embarrassing. I was sick on the train. When I got to Art School I was sick again. Oh God ... The disgrace when I told you ... you just said something like, "oh good. I'm going to be a father. Hope it's a boy, then he can go to sea too."

We married in the summer and Linda was born the following March. It was three months before you saw your daughter. You said that she was beautiful like her mother and the next one would be a boy.

I decided then that there would be no more children. The sea was my rival. I wasn't going to lose a son to that way of life.

I stayed at home. I felt tied down by the tiny bundle of noise and nappies. My Mum and Dad were captivated and did all they could to help me.

I resented your freedom Anthony. I hated the sea for taking you away from me. I was glad when my Mother suggested that I go back to Art School and she and my Aunt would look after Linda.

I got back into the swing of things, my painting improved. Linda became a little more interesting, but I counted the weeks and days till you would come home to me.

I take another sip of brandy. Dawn is blushing peach and pink all over the hills at the start of a new day. The river is calm and reflective.

The number of times I used to stand here when it was stormy, watching the water boiling and spitting in unleashed fury. The wind howling like lost souls and the rain slashing down.

I used to wonder where in the world you were. For those in peril on the sea, were words which continually echoed round my brain.

The phone rings, shrilly blasting any other thoughts from my head. I reach over and lift the receiver it's Linda.

"Hi Mum, thought I'd give you a buzz. I knew you would be up. Are you painting yet?"

"No ... I'm having a brandy ... and thinking." I was slightly annoyed at being interrupted from my reverie.

"You artist people are weird. Go easy on the booze it doesn't help. Are you OK?"

"Yes Linda I'm OK. I don't make a habit of the brandy ... I'm going to make coffee shortly. Tell me why are you phoning? Anything wrong?"

"No, no ... Just to let you know I'm at the house in Provence. It's nice and quiet with Gran and Granps away on the cruise. Why don't you come over, I'll be there for a week then I'm off to Paris with Yves."

"Yves? Is he there now?"

"I'll explain later Mum. Come over. You can paint all day, and I'm sure there is one person who would be pleased to see you. Let me know. Bye."

Yes, it is worth a thought. The light, the colours ... yes I could paint .. and Claude? I don't know ... Yes I think I'll go over.

I shower and dress. I make a mug of coffee and take it back into the den. Well if I decide I'm going away I must finish throwing out what is not needed. Right, get started then.

I start to rummage in my cupboard more old photographs. At dances, parties and on our little cabin cruiser. Your pride and joy Anthony. You had always said, that when we got our own home and had saved some money, then you would buy a boat.

You made good money. I had a few commissions, we were doing alright. Mum and Dad had retired south, they had also bought a little house in Provence so we always had holidays and they didn't cost us.

We settled into a routine. You went to sea. You came home. The first week was always wonderful. We spent every minute of every day and night together. The next week, you were restless as ever, and had to get on board your little cabin cruiser.

I often went with you and our friends to Tighnabruaich for the weekend. We were a happy crowd of people. I am sorry I couldn't go with you all the time, my commissions often ruled that out.

Fragments of your conversation drift into my head. "You know Elizabeth, you are getting too serious. I thought artists were always fun loving people. You seem to be like a pebble stuck in the sand. Nobody picks it up, and the sea washes over it."

I was stunned by that Anthony. Our emotions did ebb and flow. We were flotsam and jetsam drifting perilously towards the rocks, then being lifted high on a wave, out to sea again.

Oh damn you all those marine clichés.

When you were away and the boat was berthed at the marina I used to go on board to paint. You told me to do that, then you used to complain because I had left paints and turps lying around.

You were careless Anthony. You dropped cigarette ends which were still burning. You often drank too much gin. I suppose you didn't know what you were drinking after a while.

My best friend thought I should know what else you were up to Anthony. Why? The sea was your mistress. Why did you need another one? I never said a word about it I coped. I carried on as usual.

Sorry she was with you ... sorry about her, but she didn't know did she? The sea was your only love. Well, you got your wish. You set off on a burning boat for Valhalla ... Water under the bridge now. Oh God! What a hackneyed phrase.

I unlock a box file. One last look before I tear it all up. I lift out the newspaper and smile as I look at a picture of myself. The words printed above it leap out at me. MURDER – VERDICT – NOT PROVEN.

TEA WITH THE GRAND DUCHESS

DISCIPULI PICTURAM SPECTATE.

This phrase was my first introduction to Latin which I relished, even though I found the declensions more than a little tricky.

I learned history through this language, about the might of the Roman Empire, the Etruscans and the ancient world. I think that is when I first fell in love with Italy.

Now here I am in Florence in August, a day when the city is at her most sultry and oppressive. I have just stepped out of the cool shadowy rooms of the Pitti Palace and I need some liquid caffeine.

Oh good I see a vacant table at the little cafe across the street. I quicken my step and plonk myself down on a blue cushioned seat, just ahead of two camera laden Japanese tourists.

Immediately a waiter is at my side. I order. "*Si, con limone.*" He gesticulates, only the Italians can make an opera out of asking for a pot of tea. That is one of the reasons I love this country.

I push my sunglasses down from the fashionable top of

the head position. Now I am protected from the glare, and predatory Italian males. I can relax and drink in the history that is all around me.

I look towards the grim walls of the sixteenth century palace that I have just visited. It is a sinister place where ghosts still lurk in every dark corner.

The guide did grudgingly mention Bianca Cappello. Yes, she had been the Grand Duchess of Tuscany, but she was nothing better than a courtesan. I tried to ask more questions about her but he muttered something in Italian and walked away.

They still hate her. He denied all knowledge of where she is buried. Poor woman, maybe she was misjudged, maybe not. She certainly led a chequered life, and the Florentines blamed her for everything that went wrong in the city.

It is difficult to find much information about her, but there is a portrait of her in the Pitti Gallery and other one in the Uffizi.

What else does it say, I flick through my guide book.

November 1563, when she was only sixteen, she ran away with her lover Pietro Buonaventura. He was a Florentine, but not as he claimed, a son of the banking family Salviati. He was a son of one of the agents of the bank and had been sent to Venice to gain employment and to learn the business.

Bianca was a noblewoman from a good Venetian family. When she was only twelve her mother died, leaving her a dowry and some jewels. When Bianca eloped she took the jewels with her, but of course the family still had her dowry.

Her father re-married and his new wife perhaps jealous of Bianca's reddish gold hair and her beauty, restricted her outings, and also banished her to a separate wing of the grand mansion.

The poor girl was isolated and bored till she met Pietro. I suppose she loved Pietro. He was a handsome dark eyed young man, but he was also a means of escape from an arranged marriage.

I bring myself back to the present and pour another cp of tea. Imagine having to marry a person that I didn't love. I think I would have run away too.

Her father insisted that she was to marry a man who was the Doge's Councillor and Guardian of St Mark's Basilica. A man who had been already married and whose family were in the same age group as Bianca.

When she ran away with her lover, she had insulted her family. Charges were brought against her for defying parental authority, but absconding. She had taken her jewels with her, that was theft and she was also guilty of fornication.

The penalty for all of those crimes was that she be locked up in a nunnery for the rest of her life. Pietro was charged with seducing a noblewoman of Venice, and his penalty was death.

The Cappello family, anxious to avenge their honour, offered a reward of an exceptional amount for Pietro. This reduced the lovers to living in heavily barricaded lodgings, in constant fear of being killed by cut throats hired by the family to carry out vengeance.

This was a normal family: blood ties, feuds and killing of their own family members, supposedly to satisfy honour. Good excuse. They just got rid of whoever displeased them. I look over again at the Pitti Palace. It seems to stare back at me with a malevolent smile.

The atmosphere is full of intrigue from the centuries, unseen eyes watching the tourist tribes tramping back and forth. Are you there Bianca?

It is not entirely clear how she first me Francesco de Medici. The romanticised Italian version says that she, heavily pregnant, was walking on the Ponte Vecchio one day when Francesco saw her from a window. She looked up, their eyes met and they fell in love.

The more down to earth version implies that Bianca and Pietro entrusted themselves to Prince Francesco, by means of intermediaries, begging him to intercede with the Cappello family, and bestow his protection on them.

This was done. The couple were officially introduced into court circles. Bianca appeared among the palace ladies and Pietro was in charge of the Prince's linen. The couple had now been secretly married and their baby girl Pelligrina had been born in July 1564.

Bianca and Francesco had become lovers, not that this worried Pietro. He abused his position at court, he was a waster and a reckless and confirmed womaniser. He was murdered in 1572 by a relative of one of his lovers.

Bianca was implicated. Was she involved? Could be, or did Francesco give the order, he certainly knew that it was about to happen. Pietro was becoming an embarrassment to both of them, also to the city.

The murder just added to the hatred of Bianca by the Florentines. They called her that Venetian whore, a witch, a sorceress who had beguiled their prince.

None of this made any difference to the relationship of Bianca and Francesco, nor did the fact that he was trapped in an arranged marriage with Joanna, daughter of the Emperor of Austria.

In 1574 Cosimo, Grand Duke of Tuscany died. He was succeeded by his son Francesco, who was a quiet cultured and intelligent man. His brother Cardinal Ferdinando became a little closer to him in the hope of gaining favours, as the two brothers had never got on with each other.

The Cardinal disapproved of his relationship with Bianca. In his eyes she was bad for Florence or did he just fancy her himself or had she rebuffed him? It's all possible.

Mmm ... time I was going. Up you get and join the rest of humanity. Whew. It's hot ... hot as Dante's Inferno. I wonder how often Bianca walked here, or was possible carried on a litter. I could do with one of those.

She really was a woman of destiny, this daughter of the Venetian Republic. If she had never met Pietro, would she have married Francesco and become Grand Duchess of Tuscany after his wife died in childbirth?

Was she an adventuress? Was it ever in her mind to hook a man from one of the most powerful families in Tuscany?

Where are all these tourists coming from and must they all be on the Ponte Vecchio now, when I want to stop and stare. I push my way to a shop doorway. No don't look at all that lovely jewellery.

I stand and look up at the windows of the Vasari corridor which linked the Palazzo Vecchio with the Palazzo Pitti and passing through the Ponte Vecchio. I can almost see Francesco's long face and sad eyes staring down at me.

This passage was built so that the Medici could move safely and in secret. In fact during the last war even the Germans did not know about it.

I move further along the bridge and stand looking down at the green water and across to the coloured buildings on the Lungomare.

Oh what a city this is, and has always been rich, cultured and sophisticated. In Renaissance times when Bianca was alive, many of the great artists came here to paint. They valued the colours, the light and of course always the beautiful people.

Even today I notice people who look as if they had stepped straight out of a painting.

The streets are named after the great families and the trades, like street of the hosiers, street of the glove makers, etc. Florence was also the financial capital of the separate states at that time.

One last look at that window, where centuries ago a man looked at a woman and thereby began a notorious love story.

In October 1587 Bianca and Francesco retired to their villa in the country at Poggio a Calano. They wanted a little peace and quiet but death came suddenly to Francesco and a few hours later to Bianca. Both of them had died of bad air. Mal ... aria.

That was the official explanation but many rumours surfaced. It is known that Francesco's brother, the Cardinal was in the vicinity at that time. He was jealous of his brother and hated Bianca, and she hated him.

One story says that Bianca had prepared a poison tart for Cardinal Ferdinando and that Francesco had eaten it by mistake, horrified, Bianca had committed suicide.

I believe, as most people do that the Cardinal arranged the double murder. He had the most to gain, as after the deaths, he gave up the church and became the next Grand Duke.

It is known that he did order the body of Bianca to be taken and buried away from her husband and the Medici family. Her body is believed to be at rest in an unmarked grave in the parish of San Lorenzo.

The mystery of how Bianca and Francesco died has been a vexed question for centuries. In 1945 the tomb was opened yet again at the request of an anthropologist.

As recently as 2006 the University of Florence reported that forensic and toxicology evidence of arsenic poisoning in a study published by the British Medical Journal was the cause of death and not malaria as first thought.

It is fascinating that after all that time they can prove how a person died. It is said that arsenic may slow down the putrefaction of a body, therefore sometimes bodies exhumed after centuries can be found in a mummified condition. This would appear to be the case when they examined the viscera of Francesco and Bianca. So who murdered them? Rumours say it was Francesco's brother the Cardinal or was it the Cappello family at last avenging the family honour. Only the dead know the answer.

Back to the present and put my notes in my bag and leave the cafe. I walk to the end of the long street. I turn left into a side street and enter a small cafe. My husband greets me with "Well what did you buy?"

"Nothing, tomorrow all day shopping, but today I have just taken tea with the Grand Duchess."

THE FEMALE OF THE SPECIES

Joanna watched the orange flames lick around the guy, slowing turning him to a dark melting mass. Someone threw a firework into the blaze. It exploded, sending sparks shooting into the air, and in that split second, she knew what she must do.

The wood hissed and crackled and spat at her, the flames greedily devoured the head of the guy, licking the lips with a red hot ferocity. She could almost smell burning flesh.

She bit her lip tasting blood, what if? The guy disappeared in a pyramid of sparkling heat and flame. She smiled. It would be a terrible accident.

David's voice and a peck on the cheek startled her. "Darling, there you are, sorry I'm late. Super bonfire. Where are the others?"

"I don't know, I was looking for you."

Children jostled around shouting to each other, "look the guy is all burned up and dead."

"All burned up and dead," Joanna laughed.

"Don't be so morbid darling, let's go straight over to Louise and Bill's. I'm sure they will all be there."

"Alright David, if you say so."

Bill greeted them at the door, "Come in, O most perfect couple."

Joanna grimaced. 'If only you knew.'

"Come on, don't be modest." Bill said as he turned towards the others. "a toast to the Perfect Couple, both good looking, both successful ... and they hold the best dinner parties in the area. AND ... we're all going to their Anniversary Party next month. Drinks on the house folks. Cheers."

There was a lot of laughter and drink spilling. Bill kissed Joanna. David kissed Louise, and swung her off her feet, round and round, till they were both dizzy and fell to the floor in a giggling heap.

Joanna turned away in disgust, edging her way to the back of the room.

"I see you don't have a drink, can I get one for you?" Richard peered anxiously at her.

"Oh... I ... no ... I just ..." she shrugged.

"Wait here, smile, keep smiling, I'll be back in a sec." He returned bearing a large G&T.

"Thank you Richard." she said, taking a quick slurp from the glass.

Suddenly David was at her side. "Darling I've missed you. Dance with me." He took her hand and led her across the room. He bellowed to Bill. "A jump up and down dance. Let's have a bit of life in here."

Joanna faced David, a fixed smile on her face. She went through the motions of dancing. When the music stopped David slipped an arm round her waist.

"Did I tell you how devastating you look in black, it goes so well with your blonde hair. Devastating, but so unimaginative, and not just your dress sense. See you later." Hew blew her a kiss and walked away.

Joanna smiled a tight little smile. She was developing a headache, but she was determined to carry on.

Eventually the party ended and they got home.

"Night cap?" David slurred, as he staggered into the house.

"No thank you ... just as well Richard called a taxi for us." Joanna said quietly.

"Good old Richard, always looking after you," he mocked.

"Can I do anything for you?"

"My dear Joanna, you could never do anything for me. I'm going to the spare room to cuddle the gin bottle. Good night."

Joanna wandered into the den, switched on the small table lamp, and sat down in her favourite armchair. The central heating was full on, but she was icy cold. Her hands were shaking as she lit a cigarette, she inhaled deeply and settled further back into the chair.

Was it just three years ago since her father had introduced her to the new partner, David Blackmore? He was tall and slim, with blond hair and craggy features. When his blazing blue eyes had met hers, it was love at first sight.

They had married two months later, despite her father's misgivings. Her mother on the other hand, had been delighted to plan a wedding.

Joanna sighed, but they had been happy till about six months ago. She had called in unexpectedly at David's office, to find his personal assistant Linda just a little bit flustered and agitated. There was something about the way they had looked at each other.

She was certain that her perfect husband was having an affair with her. She was good looking in a sluttish sort of way, masses of black hair and lashings of eye make up.

Joanna began to tremble with a mixture of rage and pity

for herself. "Bastard." she spat out the word, tears stinging her eyes.

From the moment she had met him, she had put him on a pedestal, so was she to blame? He was master in his own house, wasn't that what a man wanted? Although a strong personality herself in her own business, she had pandered to his every whim at home.

She had ignored the little doubts that rumbled about her brain. An ideal husband, no such thing. Oscar Wilde was correct in his assumption that, it is a weakness in women, when they must see their man as ideal. But she despised weak men. Her father wasn't weak, and Richard, when his wife died, he wasn't weak.

Another thought flitted into her mind. David had married the boss's daughter. The social portcullis had been lifted for him. He really was not her type. He was more akin to Linda, political views and all.

Would children have made a difference? No. Neither of them wanted them. Now she would have to admit to her father, that once again he was right and she was wrong.

She had a successful career in marketing, but despite that, she never felt that she had her father's approval. Her father had longed for a son, but had produced a daughter. That wasn't her fault. She had her father's strong personality, and she proved to him that she was his equal in business. Now she had to admit that she was a failure where marriage was concerned. She would phone him in the morning.

David's voice wakened her, "Morning, you are going to be late for business, tut, tut, we can't have that. Don't wait up for me tonight ... I ... eh may not be home. Bye."

Joanna swore under breath. She lifted the phone and dialled her father's number. Within twenty minutes she was showing him into the den. She silenced his questions with

"Father, for once, just listen to me. This is not easy. I ... I want you to get a private detective on David."

"I've already done that, and it's bad news. I'll leave you this with you. Phone me when you need to talk."

"Thank you Father ... I ... I really am grateful." Her father ran his fingers through his immaculate silver hair. "I think I should warn you that ..."

"NO, don't tell me anything. I'll deal with it." Her father nodded, and left the house.

Joanna phoned her office feigning sickness. She poured herself a glass of brandy, and settled down in her chair in the den.

She took two large sips of brandy and told herself, that it was better that she know now what was on the tape.

She pressed the button, and the video whirred into action. It was a gardening programme, it must be the wrong film. The garden was familiar in its summer glory. Yes. It was Ann's birthday party, in June. The camera panned round lots of well known faces including her own.

The next shot was in the rose garden. The camera moved in unashamedly on a couple who were wrapped together in a passionate embrace. Joanna's blood screamed through her veins. It was David and Louise. Joanna ran into the bathroom and was violently sick.

Eventually she got up, went into the kitchen, poured herself a glass of soda water, and decided to get on with the rest of the video.

It got worse and worse. David and Linda in compromising positions in the office. David leaving Louise's house the week that Bill was away on business.

She didn't blame Linda, she was obviously flattered, but Louise, that was something else. Joanna laughed aloud at the very nasty plan that was forming in her mind.

She phoned David's office. Linda answered, and told her

that David had gone to London and would not be back till tomorrow. Linda agreed to visit Joanna on her way home.

It didn't take long to tell Linda the sordid details. It had almost been a pleasure to watch her face turn paler and paler as she watched the video. Her outburst of anger would have done a trooper proud. She agreed to everything Joanna suggested.

David continued to work late. Joanna continued to work late. They hardly saw each other. Soon it was the evening of their anniversary party and everything seemed to be going well. David was proposing a toast to Joanna. "To my beautiful, wonderful wife, may we have many more years together." He kissed her.

"You know you don't like champagne darling," she said.

"Get me a G&T then old girl."

"Certainly pet, last one before the bonfire alright?"

Joanna went into the kitchen, poured a large gin into a glass, removed the phial from its secret place, and emptied the contents into the drink. She was humming to herself as she added ice, lemon and tonic.

"Here you are darling," she handed the drink to David who grabbed it from her. "Hope there's plenty of gin in it, not like your usual, all tonic and no gin."

She watched as he took a gulp. She smiled at him, a cold chilling smile. Never mind the dash of gin, enjoy the dash of atropine, you bastard.

"Time for the bonfire, the ceremonial lighting up." David bellowed as he lurched towards the door. Joanna darted towards him.

"Darling, why don't I come with you and we'll light the bonfire together?"

"NO, I am the master of this house, I, do it alone." he roared as he staggered off, drink in hand, to the bottom of the garden.

"I ... I ... don't know ... we ..." Joanna mumbled. Someone said "Let's stay indoors." They crowded round the large window and peered into the darkness.

It all happened as Joanna planned. David must have stumbled when he bent over the light the bonfire. He had lain there in his drunken state for about five minutes before anyone had realised that anything was wrong.

Joanna played the grieving widow well enough to gain an Oscar for her performance. Louise. She couldn't quite make up her mind what to do about her. She might show her the video sometime, but meanwhile it amused her to remain friends with her.

Joanna had inherited her father's business. She was ruthlessly efficient. Linda was still studying law, still married to her rich old husband, who was a very jealous man. If he ever found out about David, who knows what would happen.

How could she explain what she was doing, standing behind the bonfire that night. And she was on tape, saying that it had only taken a little push. Joanna had her totally in her power. In actual fact, they got on rather well, as long as Linda remembered that Joanna was the boss.

Then, there was Richard. She always knew that he would do anything for her, and he had. He was a big noise in the University lab, he had provided the atropine. He was becoming a bit of a nuisance, he wanted to marry her.

Joanna thought about his continual proposals. What a bore and just when she was getting on rather well with Phillipe from the Paris office. She would have to do something about Richard.

THE THOUGHTS OF JAMIE (AGED 2 ½ YEARS)

"Are you singing a wee song? Yes you are." A large female shape looms over the baby in the next parking place beside me. The baby gurgles as she tickles his dribbling chin till her hand is wet.

Silly lady, how can he sing a song, he is only a baby. There she goes again, "Coochie coochie coo." The baby's mum comes into the room. She thanks the large lady and tells her how grateful she is for the crèche.

She points to her head and says something about having a bad hair day. I don't understand. How can her hair be bad?

Mummies may be pleased that they can leave us here for ages while they do the shopping. Ok so we have privileged parking and we are looked after, but it's a bit much having to put up with all the goo's, smiling to order and the wee songs.

Oh no. It's my turn, here she comes, beaming all over. "It's James isn't it? What a bi … iig boy. You are fairly growing." Well that's what I am supposed to do, and considering all the yucky stuff I have to eat. No wonder I am growing.

"Don't want you getting too big, do we?"

Oh give me a break. I am only two and a half, and I am only James when mummy is angry with me.

"Mmmuumm." I whimper.

"Wee story?"

Oh no, can she not be more original?

"You're a lovely bouncing boy."

So I am, a bouncing boy, but boys are not lovely. Bouncy. bouncy, bouncy, I bounce all the more. Babysitters hate that, it frightens them.

"No dear, no ... oh."

I let out an ear shattering yell and bounce more furiously.

"NO, bad boy."

I lean over the side of the push chair and shake and bounce.

"You are a very bad boy,"

"Mmmmuuumm ... mm ... mmm." I whimper with just enough pathos.

"There, mummy is coming pet." she pats my arm Ok, now for the favourite, the shaky petted lip. that always drives them bats. "Mmmmmm." I gasp.

"Oh dear, a wee petted lip." I do my best to bring up wind. "Mummy's coming."

"MMMMMUUUUMM."

"Oh dear dear wee laddie." She pulls my wee woolly bunnet further over my eyes.

"Is that it, are you wee ears cold?"

I shake my head vigorously in an effort to see. That doesn't work. I lift my podgy little hand to my head.

"No, you musn't be a naughty boy. Oh you can't see wee man, alright. What lovely brown eyes you have and, is that dark hair?"

"Mmmuumm."

"Clever boy. You can see Mum, but I am not your Mum."

I know that. My Mum is in the supermarket. I'm fed up.

Well now for the red face and the constipation struggle. "AAAAAHH." I squawk, trying to look awful. Now to raise the decibel level "AAAAAAHH"

"My goodness nothing wrong with your lungs." She moves the pushchair back and forward like Daddy when he cuts the grass. Right. That's it. I throw my teddy bear at her and give the loudest yell ever.

I contort my face with rage and go up the scale. "AAAAAAAAAAAHH."

"Shhhhhh. Mummy's coming, there, there." She picks up Teddy. I throw him back at her.

"Naughty boy, poor Teddy." She cuddles him would you believe it. He's only a toy and she cuddles him. I cuddle him when I am in bed, but he is mine.

Where is Mummy? I know she is shopping, but she has been away for a long time. I don't think I'll go shopping when I grow up, unless it's for toys.

"Oh, you're a pretty girl aren't you?"

It's the round one again, speaking to a little girl. Ugh. She's sitting up in a multi colour stroller. That's a pram.

I look at the little doll with the blonde curls and the china blue eyes. She is sitting up straight, although she is strapped in. Now she is doing her best to bounce. A girl bouncing?

"Gooo, gooo, goo." she says pouting at me and chuckling. Goo. Goo. What does that mean? Girl Talk. She stretches out her little dimpled fingers "Gooooo."

The round one turns to me, "Look at that lovely little lady. She knows how to behave." At that point little Miss Curly Top leans over her pram and tries to give me her pink bunny rabbit. "Goo. Goo. Da da."

She has a glint in her eye as she smiles at me "Goooo" I glare at her "Aaaaaahh" I bawl.

"Now that's not very nice, say Hullo to the little girl. Her name is Caroline."

I scowl. "Aaaaahh."

"OH we are in a little mood aren't we?" She turns to the little girl. Good. Wish my Mummy would hurry up. I'm fed up waiting. When she comes back I'm going to play up something terrible.

I hate it in here. It was better sitting in the trolley being pushed about. I felt like a little Prince in his little chariot. I could see what was happening.

When Mummy stopped I could lift things and drop them. I could scream and yell and no amount of shooshing would shut me up. Sometimes Mummy would be so embarrassed she would have to take me out.

I tried it on Daddy and lots of ladies tried to quieten me, but I yelled as loud as I could and Daddy had to take me out.

Hope Mum remembers I prefer Pampers for boys and not the unisex things for girls and boys.

After all little boys have extra bits that little girls don't have, so I want BOY Pampers.

Hope she gets some decent food, like crisps and Irn Bru and chocolate, then I'll be sick and make a mess.

I like when Granny takes me to MacDonalds for a special meal. I have chicken nuggets or hamburger and chips with ketchup. I see all my friends and we have a nice chat over a coca cola. And Granny is great fun.

"Goooo. goooo. goooo." Can a boy baby not get any peace from Girl babies. "She really is pretty I smile. "Ehhh O." I say in my best Telly tubby voice. "Mmmmm" she scowls.

"Ehhh O Lala" screeches a little dark haired girl in the pink push chair. She is smiling at me. Ohhhh. She is nice. I try to stand up and get out of my chair. She gurgles and tries to grab my arm.

I lean towards her and topple out of my pram, head first. I let out a loud yell. My head hurts. I really am crying now. Little Miss Brunette is laughing.

The round one hurries over and picks me up. "There, there, that will teach you not to show off in front of the girls. Be a big brave boy and stop crying, Boys don't cry. Only little girls cry."

I scream all the louder.

I hate girls.

THE SENIOR PARTNER

Hilary could vaguely hear the traffic starting to move, one car, then another, then silence, then more traffic noise. The light was just filtering through the ruched curtain as she struggled to the surface, dragging herself through the sleep barrier, into total consciousness. Her eyelids felt so heavy, she was convinced that they were stuck together with heavy duty glue.

Her head felt like a concrete block. She squinted at the clock, till at last she gained full focus. Yes, it was six thirty. Time to get up. After three attempts, she sat up. Her head was going to fall off. She had never felt so bad, not even when she had been a student at law school, and there had been parties and lots of cheap plonk. She wanted to die.

Something was very wrong. What a bubbling cauldron of a hangover this was. This must surely be more than an excess of alcohol. She felt sick again.

She swung her legs over the bed. The room swayed and moved, and turned. You can do it she told herself, as she gritted her teeth. She stood up, and another wave of nausea engulfed her. She prided herself on the fact that she had suffered many a hangover, and still arrived for business, the morning after the night before.

Not today old girl, she thought as she ran the shower. She turned it off. Oh No, too dangerous, must get back to bed. The room was revolving all around her. She sank down into her bed. Her head ached, her limbs ached, her mouth was fuzzy. The office can do without me she decided.

She looked at the glass of milk which Geoffrey had left on the bedside table. He had said that it was his best cure for a hangover. Dear sweet Geoffrey. He had brought her home, undressed her and put her to bed.

He told her to drink the milk, and she would feel better in the morning.

She had been too ill to resist, as Geoffrey held the glass to her lips she took a few mouthfulls. He had then put the glass down on her bedside table, when she had promised him that she would drink the rest of it later.

He did not stay that night, as he had to catch an early flight to Paris in the morning. She had been too ill to want him to stay anyway.

The phone rang shattering the silence, and splintering her brain. It was Geoffrey, the darling. He was so worried about her. Yes, he was at the airport. She assured him that she was recovering, and hung up.

Oh how awful, she felt. She was hot, although the hammering in her head was easing she still felt sick.

Oh, NO, No, No, she just could not be pregnant, could she? Don't be silly she told herself, everything was normal.

She tossed and turned, and finally fell asleep. She woke in a panic, sweating profusely, the office, the interview! God, it was mid-day. She had to get to the office. Her interview for the partnership was vital to her.

She got up, and when she had showered, she felt slightly more human. She dressed with care in a neat black suit, with a knee length skirt, which showed her long slim legs to perfection. A white silk blouse, a pearl choker, and pearl stud ear-rings completed the business look.

She sat down at the dressing table, and flicked her long black hair into style. She stared at the dark smudges beneath her brown eyes. God, what a mess she looked. Her hand was shaking as she applied her make-up.

She was still dizzy, but she was determined. She stood up, this partnership meant so much to her. She had been with the firm for only five years, and now, to be on the short list at age thirty!

She made herself a mug of tea, and sat down. There was plenty of time, her interview was at three o'clock. What a party last night, a celebration of fifty years, as a family law business. She had danced all night with a variety of men, including Geoffrey's father, Nicholas Fenshaw.

A pleasant man, tall, dark, fairly good looking, with quite an understated charm. He had the most gorgeous eyes, hazel, with flecks of green. Hilary smiled, yes, she noticed his eyes, as they stared into hers, when he held her close, as they were dancing. Sometimes Hilary thought that she liked him better than Geoffrey. He was approachable when she had any problems at the office.

She felt sorry for him too. He had married Lisbeth when she was pregnant with Geoffrey. He was not Geoffrey's father, but had brought him up as his own, till at the age of eighteen, he had told him the truth.

His father was an Austrian ski instructor, that Lisbeth had a fling with, while she was engaged to Nicholas. She still played around even after they married, and eventually ran off with an Argentinian polo player. As far as anyone knows, they still live in South America.

Something began to niggle at the back of Hilary's mind. It concerned Geoffrey. It was not just the fact that he and

Gloria Stevens, had been wrapped together, time after time on the dance floor, last night. She had excused him on the grounds that he couldn't hold his alcohol and that Gloria was a bit of a tease, and that she, Hilary was engaged to him.

No, there was something else. Someone had said something last night, that had disturbed her but she couldn't remember what it was. She drank another cup of tea and swallowed two aspirins. She wanted this partnership, she was capable.

Geoffrey did not seem too keen about it, stating that he would take over the firm anyway, when his father retired. When he spoke of the man he called his father, it was always in a sarcastic tone. He envied him, and hated him at the same time. Hilary was always annoyed when he decried Nicholas, after all, Geoffrey's mother was the wrong doer. Geoffrey did not seem to see it that way, he approved of everything his mother did.

Hilary rang for a taxi, and reached the office with about twenty minutes to spare. Judy at reception greeted her with "Oh Mr Fenshaw said you wouldn't be in today. Are you feeling better?"

The interview was conducted by Nicholas Fenshaw, and the other two senior partners. It lasted for one hour, and Hilary was more than relieved when it was over. As Nicholas showed her out, he said quietly "I hope you are feeling better."

She left immediately, and walked through the park to her flat. The fresh air had cleared her head, and she felt much better. As she entered the flat, she heard the telephone ringing, but she was too late to answer it.

She made herself a pot of tea, and as she let it infuse, a troublesome thought crossed her mind. Why had Geoffrey phoned the office to say that she would definitely not be attending the interview? What was he playing at? She poured herself a cup of tea, and flopped on to the sofa.

Sometimes she saw the dark side of Geoffrey's character. He was a taker, and a charmer. He was tall with blond hair, and denim blue eyes. She had been bowled over by him. Friends had warned her, that he was a Jeckyll and Hyde, and not at all a nice person. She knew all that, but she didn't care.

As a lover, he was unique, passionate, yet tender, always exciting, all she had ever wanted. When she mentioned the partner's job, he had become so sarcastic, and shown such a cruel ruthless streak, that Hilary wondered if she did love him.

The shrill sound of the door bell cut through her thoughts. She answered the call, to find Nicholas Fenshaw framed in the doorway.

"Thank heavens you're alright," he murmured.

"Eh, yes" she stammered.

"Hilary," he began, "I phoned, and when you didn't answer, I thought I'd come right over ... I ... I was worried about you. Congratulations, you are my new senior partner."

"Oh ... I'm, Hilary burst into tears.

Nicholas sat down beside her, "I take it you are happy about it?"

"Oh, yes, yes," she sobbed.

He put his arms around her, and gently pulled her to his chest. Hilary began to tremble, she stopped sobbing.

"I'll make some tea," she said leaping up quickly.

"Please don't, I , I must get back to the office, I just ..."

He turned to face her at the door, his hazel eyes looking at her with such depth of feeling, that she was almost hypnotised. He shook her hand, leant forward, and kissed her lightly on the lips, "See you tomorrow, partner."

As she closed the door, she began to tremble again. Nicholas had kissed her, and she had wanted him to do so.

She sat down. Oh what a mix up. She had to admit, she did find Nicholas very attractive. Over the past year, they seemed to have grown close. They agreed over the same things in business, shared a joke here and there, and generally got on well together.

Geoffrey had been a bit peeved on one occasion, when she and Nicholas had to work together, through a Friday and Saturday. She had to admit to herself, that the Friday had not been a problem. They had worked hard all day, straight through till about nine. He had put her in a taxi, and sent her home.

On the Saturday, they had worked till about seven thirty, when Nicholas suggested dinner. She had protested, but they had ended up in a romantic little restaurant in Soho. It had been a very pleasant evening, but they both had had too much to drink. They had enjoyed each others company. Something had happened between them, which they both chose to ignore. They took a taxi back to her flat, but she entered the flat alone.

Geoffrey had gone on about his father, trying to make Hilary feel indebted to him for dinner. Indebted, the alarm bells were ringing in her head ... indebted . Debt ... that was it! Last night at the party, she had walked into the powder room, just in time to hear part of a conversation about Geoffrey, and his gambling debts. She would ask him outright, when he returned from Paris, debts, and Gloria Stevens!

She undressed and slipped into bed, she could not sleep, all sorts of thoughts tumbled about in her mind. Nicholas ... the feel of his arms about her. No, No, No, she was engaged to Geoffrey, she was the new senior partner, that was what she wanted.

She finally dozed off, but awoke with a start.

What was that noise? She heard a key turn in the outside

door. She switched on the light, scrambled out of bed, into the hall.

"Who is that? Geoffrey? What?"

"Yes darling, it's me," his voice was low and silky, his eyes were staring."I had to come back, there's something I must do."

His voice changed, "Sit down Hilary." It was an angry command. Hilary was desperately trying to remain calm, but her heart was thudding, and she was scared.

"What's wrong Geoffrey, why are you here, You ... you, should still be in Paris."

He stared at her coldly, "Do you really care?"

He sat down beside her, his eyes like cold blue ice, his mouth twisted in an evil smile.

"What?" she faltered.

"Shut up," he roared, as he struck her across the face.

"Oh my God," Hilary screamed, her stomach lurched, she began to shake.

He pulled her towards him, and kissed her roughly. She struggled, "Geoffrey ... what?"

He hit her again, and she stumbled, "Shut up!" he hissed.

"Listen to me Hilary," his voice changed again, seductive, and deep. "You must drink your milk, this time, then I'm going to kill you, slowly, with pleasure." He laughed, a shrill, insane laugh. Hilary cowered against the wall, Oh God, he's mad, he means it. He was chalk white, his eyes staring at her, like an animal going for the kill.

Drink milk ... kill her ... she looked at his face, set like granite. HE DID MEAN IT! Oh my God! Hilary knew she had to try and remain calm. She felt a chill run down her spine, her mouth was dry, her breathing was erratic. She felt she was going to faint. Her whole being was on red alert. She had to escape, but first she had to hold his attention.

He spoke again, his voice as brittle, and cold as shattered

ice. "You ... get my partnership ... I get nothing, till after my father retires. He hates me, because I'm NOT his son. He loves you, but he won't have you. YOU ... are going away!

He grabbed her round the waist, and dragged her into the kitchen. "I'm going to make you that special milky drink ... and you're going to drink all of it." He pulled her head back and kissed her. "Aren't you!"

"Yes." she whispered.

He slid his hands round her throat and squeezed.

"If you drink your milk, it will be so easy." Hilary struggled to free herself. He released her abruptly, and began to cry, as he sank to the floor.

"Oh God, I can't do it. I drugged your drinks. I poisoned your milk. I . . I tried to smother you, but I couldn't do it then, and I can't do it now. Oh God help me! He stretched out his hand to Hilary, who moved to the doorway, out of his reach. She stared at him in disgust.

"My mother didn't want me," he screamed, "I was just the product of a careless fling. I was never wanted, never loved. You don't want me either, you just want the partnership, and Nicholas." He was rolling about the floor, sobbing like a child. "I hate Nicholas, he is everything I'm not. I hate you. I WANT MY MUMMY."

Hilary ran into the hall, opened the front door, and came face to face with Nicholas and two policemen.

She felt herself falling, falling, falling, into a black abyss.

When she came round, an anxious voice was whispering her name, over, and over again, holding her close, and kissing her hair. She opened her eyes and whispered "Nicholas, Oh Nicholas."

UTOPIA

NEW BRITANNIA
   EURO SPACE STATION
   PLANET UTOPIA
   NEAR VENUS
   SPA 16 UTO
   26 August 2018

Dear Mum & Dad,
   SWITCH ON TV – SKY SPACE CHANNEL.
   UTO EURO SCOT

Arrived safely, after one hour delay at stop over Station Zero. This was due to a very close encounter with one of the Russian space ships on patrol in our area. Onward journey was fantastic. We could see the earth, it is round. All the countries very clearly defined. It was raining in Greenock, all the way down to Ayr.

I said to Jane, "My parents are down there." She replied "So are mine." We both burst into tears and within minutes everyone else was crying too.

The flight was very smooth, and the service at dinner was good. The waiters started us off with a Silver Sparkler (Bucks Fizz) to us. Then a choice of wine, Martian Red, robust and bellicose, or Whispering White, a dry seductive wine from Venus. They served us meat and two veg. and assured us that, although the meat had traces of CJD. E. COLLI and two other virulent germs, it was perfectly safe to eat as it had been treated with moon dust.

The veg. were radio active, but we needed that to acclimatise ourselves to the new atmosphere. One wag shouted that it didn't matter as we were all crackling from all the radio activity on earth.

Jane and I are staying at the Venus Hilton, a four star space rest for women only, run by the Americans. We have a fabulous suite, everything is normal, beds, chairs, etc. fantastic materials. The bathroom is film star status, all lights and mirrors.

We are waited on hand and foot by manservants who look like the Chippendales, just as well they are robots. I'm just beginning to believe it all now. I have been accepted by the New Labour Space Commission Work Experience Dept. I am going to be in charge of Fashion for New Britannia and Jane is to be my assistant.

It was so exciting. Mrs May and Nicola Sturgeon saw us off. Both of them gave a speech and told us how privileged we were to be on the Inter Planetary Welfare to Work Scheme. We are pioneers of a brave new world and a new life style, regardless of race, colour or creed, we will go down in history and be remembered as humanitarians. Hints are being dropped all over the place that if and when Scotland becomes totally independent our place on this planet will be known as Nova Scotia.

Mrs May encouraged Nicola to visit Utopia and make sure that everything is running smoothly.

Rumour has it that Nicola will be coming to open the Utopia football stadium so that at Hogmanay Rangers and Celtic can play. The Tartan Army will arrive for this special game, but getting back to earth could be a problem for them.

We have a moon buggy to get about. It is the equivalent of "the mini". We chose a silver stunner, souped up model. We also have a scooter each which is part of our exercise regime outwith the gym.

We have signed up for five years because everything is new and life will never be dull.

I have lots of ideas. I am going to start a Come Dancing class and a competition. I have already opened a Writers' Club and have several members. We communicate every Wednesday evening with my club on earth and some of the members wish to visit soon. I look forward to that.

I have brought my paints etc., with me so that is next on my bucket list.

News Flash – Donald Trump will make a visit to Utopia. He wants to build a golf course, a Las Vegas type hotel and a housing estate for special friends. Trump Utopia.

A new TV series is being filmed here at the moment, Rebus in Utopia, also NY Police Dept. Blue Bloods in space. Best news of all, DR WHO will be played this time by a woman.

There is a rumour that certain well known people are being held in the Tower of London till it is time for their flight to Utopia. Mrs May, Jeremy Corbyn, Alec Salmond, and the top people in the French, Belgian and German Governments. In a leaked letter from No 10 it has become apparent that the people on this list may have difficult returning to earth.

Oops, nearly forgot, extra people on this list, David & Victoria Beckham and perhaps Nicola Sturgeon.

We live under cover of a giant glass dome. The air is purified, but it is possible to walk outside the dome for a shot time, wearing all the gear, of course.

The weather is controlled. We still have the four seasons, but no extremes of temperature. Solar heat is used when necessary. Night and daylight is adjusted to our needs.

Colours in sky space are fantastic. Moonlight takes on a new meaning. The stars, sorry planets, really do twinkle.

It's funny to see mechanical cats and dogs. The Animal Rights people raised objections to the real thing.

One of the old dears, a Brit, walks her dog in the evening, but she can't quite understand why her pet cannot raise its leg when it comes to a plastic tree. What a giggle. Now the clever people are on a project to make this possible.

It's true, honestly. We actually know this lady. You should see the dog's lead. It is red, white and blue, that is, rubies, diamonds and sapphires. Very patriotic.

Our Boutique is nearly ready. It is in the 10 star plus, plus, plus Hotel, the Clinton Cosmos. American and totally O.T.T. Frank Sinatra was supposed to do a show there, but he died.

We are calling the Boutique, Gold and Silver, as this is the colour scheme. Jane will wear a silver tinfoil mini with a low neckline and long sleeves a sprinkling of silver in her dark hair, and silver knee length thonged boots will complete the picture.

I will be dressed exactly the same, only in gold because I am blonde. The outfits are actually in a new tartan, royal blue and silver and on the opening day we will paint our faces, blue and white like the saltire. Fly the flag, wherever.

Hopefully we will be able to open another Boutique in the Braveheart Hotel when they finish building it. This hotel will outdo Gleneagles, it will be 20 star luxury.

Just imagine it, wake up to the romantic sound of bagpipes, go to the sleep to the same sound. All the tartans of all the clans used as soft furnishings and wall paper. Pictures of Rabbie and Bonnie Prince Charlie everywhere.

And Mum, they are also saying that Scotland, terrestrial Scotland that is, will be kept for huntin', shootin' and fishin' for special people. Only the central belt will have ordinary working people, whatever that means.

Oh, nearly forgot, I've been "beamed up" well, on a simulator. It was fun, just like pins and needles. Jane was scared stiff. Certainly makes the phrase "Beam me up Scotty" very appropriate.

Reminds me, thanks for the food parcel, it came yesterday by the inter galactic silver arrow, that is express service. Must have my porridge in the morning. You sent me enough to feed the planet. Did you buy out Tesco's?

Only joking, it was great to see all the goodies, frozen fish and chips, Mars Bars, Irn Bru, real bread. Maybe Jane and I will think about opening a tearoom, we could make a fortune.

They haven't perfected the water yet, so it was brilliant of you to think of sending gallons of good Scottish water to put in our good Scottish whisky.

Talking of trees, we Scots are trying to grow thistles and heather. Eventually they say, things will grow and we can have a Utopia in space flower show.

The scenery here is quite flat. The Americans are building mountains from papier machè, till they figure out how to import real rocks. They have given us plastic trees which are lifelike.

They have opened a McDonald's, selling regular Planet Fries, Mega Astra Mac and Mega Mega Galaxy Mac. It is very busy.

The French are squabbling over food quotas and threatening to blockade the shuttle ports. The Italians want new pasta machines, and they are both worried about wine imports.

The Germans who go to the Solarium are still putting their towels down on the Sun sofas. Would you believe it?

We Brits are having a hard time trying to outwit all of them. Never mind, we Scots will soon be in charge. Oh Mum, is it true that Clydeside will be building ships again, space ships that is, and the first one will be called Mary Queen of Scots?

We have been on a social whirl. Even on this planet, there is rivalry between Glasgow and Edinburgh, in the pubs.

We went to The Gallus Besom last week. It was Cosmic Karaoke night. What a laugh. The drinks are something else. There is a MEGA MAC, that's whisky and Irn Bru with a dash of brandy. MOON MAGIC, is coconut milk and rum, completed with silver palm trees and sun brolly in the glass.

Dad, you must try the beer when you come here. It's called SPACE SHOOGLE, and it's guaranteed to make you feel you have reached the outer limits.

The new cocktail is called HALLUCINATION. It is a heady mix of vodka and green chartreuse, one of them makes you see little green men climbing out of your glass.

We have joined the moon dancing group, run by the dance crazy Glaswegians. We are learning how to do the moon mambo.

The Edinburgh pub, sorry, wine bar is called, The General Assembly. It's for intellectuals and serves drinks called Reverend Rum Cocktail and Presbyterian Punch. Exchange visits between the pub and wine bar should be a barrel of laughs.

MUM a quick word about our clothes. They are real Space Age but we do a range of Earth Clothes too. They are actually becoming antiques but are much in demand for parties. So hang on to all of yours and bring them with you when you come here.

We are doing a range of Hostess Space suits in our new tartan, Clan Scotia. I'll keep one aside for you. See if Dad wants a pair of trews in the same tartan. He'll want them when he joins the Golf Club up here.

No need to worry about money. It's a sort of points system turned into money figures. You get a personal calculator which is linked to the Bank of Scotia. No problem.

They are reducing the age limit to 40 so you had better apply for your flight now although the over 45's have priority as to the 16 to 25's.

We get all the news up her before Earth. Just hear that the Special Shuttle with all THE people is due in three weeks. Have to go now, only allowed fifteen minutes on this machine. LOVE CHRISTINE XXXXXX

WHISPERS

The steam drifted lazily round the bathroom releasing the sweet scent of sandalwood. Claire sank further into the soothing water and rested her head on the little bath pillow.

Suddenly the room became cold, very cold. Claire sat up quickly, her hands gripping the sides of the bath. She could hardly breath, the pulse in her throat threatening to choke her, as the soft lighting cast dancing shadows among the swirling steam.

The tiles were closing in on her, and the full size panel of the Greek goddess was floating towards her offering a flower as she rippled through the air. Just for a moment, the goddess hovered. Now she was changing, fading, disappearing. In her place a man, smiling and whispering ... Claire.

IT WAS HIM. Just for a moment Claire felt herself floating upwards to meet him. Floating and fluttering like a butterfly, soaring free out of life. He stretched out his arms to embrace her. She slumped down into the water.

Somewhere far, far away, she heard a voice. She struggled to hear what it was saying, gradually it sounded nearer and nearer. It was John's voice. "Claire, are you asleep in there? Claire do you hear me?" He burst through the door "Claire."

"I think I nodded off, I'm ..." her voice wavered. John sighed, "Oh, well, as long as you are alright." He left the room.

She carefully climbed out of the bath. She felt odd, not in control of herself, light headed and nauseous. her heart was pounding and she was shaking. Must pull myself together, she told herself, as she dried off and wrapped herself in a white towelling robe.

"Are you alright," John asked as she came out of the bathroom.

"I think so." she nodded.

"Get this down you, and RELAX. I'm going to take a bath."

She climbed on to the bed and lay back. She took a large sip of whisky savouring its smooth taste. All sorts of thoughts were twisting and turning through the canals of her mind. What if? ... this. What if? ... that. Had she fallen asleep? Had she fainted? Was she pregnant? OH NO ... NO, she couldn't be. Then, was she heading for a breakdown?

She knew John was concerned about her, but if only he would ... He didn't really understand women, and he could not cope with illness, to him it did not exist.

She had been working very hard. She had also attended lots of functions with John, after all she was the Managing Director's wife. Sometimes their careers collided, but Claire always gave in to John's reminder that he did own the most successful small printing firm in London.

John was right, she did need to relax, and get more sleep. Her own job in advertising was a problem. She was always on a tight schedule, but she loved it, and she had done well for herself. She COULD cope, she would re-arrange her schedules, but the dreams ...

They had started last year, after her mother had died, and her father had gone to live with his mistress, only three months later. A natural re-action the doctor had told her, but was it natural to dream about death every night, death by drowning. Her mother had taken an overdose, she had not drowned.

When Claire woke from those dreams, she was always drenched in perspiration, and totally exhausted. John was very understanding at first, but as the dreams continued, he told her she was neurotic. He thought she should give up work and have a baby. She did not want a family and they argued frequently about it.

The other dreams ... she could not tell John about. How could she? They were dreams of passion, total and all consuming. She woke from them pleasantly tired and glowing with a strange happiness.

What was happening to her? Was she going to be like her mother? NO. It was her father's infidelities that had made her mother unstable, but what of her grandmother? She could not remember the details. She had once as a young girl overheard her mother and her aunt talking about her great grandmother. What was it ...

Oh that was in the past. I'm just overtired and trying to be the perfect woman, she told herself. Little tingles of anxiety were starting in the pit of her stomach. Could John be jealous of her success? Did he really want her to be an ideal stay at home wife and mother?

It will all sort itself out, she tried to convince herself. She was behaving like a juvenile, dreaming about a pop star. What an idiot she was. She was made of sterner stuff. Wasn't she?

She got up rather unsteadily, and crossed the room to the window. She stood looking out across the courtyard. The gas lamps glowed eerily through a thin veil of mist.

Her eyes travelled to the clock tower above the entrance, and then left to the stables. She shivered and then tensed. She could hear drumming hoof beats, nearer and nearer, louder and louder. A horse whinnied and whimpered, as if in pain.

The mist was spinning and dancing into sinister shapes. Soft yellow light was creeping out from the open stable door, it mingled with the mist and became the figure of a tall man. He looked up at Claire and beckoned to her. "Andrew" she gasped, and sank to the floor.

She sat for a moment, her head reeling. It WAS Andrew. Of course it was. Just like her dreams, tall, with dark tousled hair, deep, dark brown eyes, and a heart jolting smile.

She got up rather shakily. She could hardly breathe. The blood was pounding and screaming through her veins. What was happening to her?

She looked out of the window. The mist had cleared. The gas lamps glowed brightly. She started at the solid grey buildings. They stared back in insolent defiance. There was NOBODY there ... NOBODY ... NOTHING ... NOTHING to be frightened about. Was there?

She was still shaking, but she told herself not to be stupid. John was right. It was all due to stress and overwork ... and the dreams? What happened just now ... and in the bath-room? Her ghostly lover? RUBBISH ... She did not believe in ghosts. She steadied herself and poured another malt.

What was it then? The small voice of doubt nagged. Something deep in her subconscious. Was it sexual? It must be. She continually dreamt about this man ... Andrew. How did she know his name? It must have been one of the books she had read, and with all the stress ... it had come to the surface.

Was there madness in the family? Snatches of her moth-er's conversation with her aunt, drifted into her mind.

Our mad relative ... fallen in love with an Indian ... fire ... disgrace ... married off to a Lord ... Madness.

Who was it? Great Grandmother, Grandmother, Who? Had it been about falling in love with the wrong man? Falling foul of society, as it was then. Claire pondered. "Am I mad? Is it in the family?

She took another few gulps of whisky. Gradually her breathing slowed down, and she felt calmer. She decided, she was not mad, she could cope, and what she had just drunk, was amazingly good medicine. Well, she giggled, it was used as a medicine in the old days.

"Feeling better?" John emerged from the bathroom. His brown hair was plastered to his head, his blue eyes looked troubled. He was reasonably tall, and solidly built, but at this moment, to Claire, he looked like a well scrubbed schoolboy.

"Did you wash behind your ears?" Claire smiled as she embraced him, "the best medicine in the world, The Water of Life."

"What is?" John said a little impatiently.

"Whisky, that is what it is know as, here in the Highlands.

"Claire," he took her hands in his, "listen to me and don't interrupt. When we go back to London I want you to see Dr Fenwick. I'm concerned about you. I don't want you having a nervous breakdown. Will you promise to ..."

"I'm perfectly alright, just tired." she snapped.

"Fine," said John wearily.

"I'm sorry," she sighed, "I'll think about it, alright? Now let's just enjoy the week-end."

"Did you hang my suit in here?"

"I hope not, that leads to the secret stairway" Claire murmured.

"It's locked, anyway, why don't they have proper wardrobes?" he muttered opening the door to a walk in cupboard. He came out looking puzzled, "Secret stairway? How do you know that?"

"I … I must have read about in, in the brochure."

Claire toyed with her food all the way through the meal. She was on edge. She felt as if she had been plugged into the national grid. Her body was alive and sparking with excitement.

John ate heartily and drank three quarters of the bottle of wine. They didn't speak much. He seemed contents just to look at her now and then and listen to the resident pianist.

"Coffee will be served in the long gallery." said the elderly waiter staring at Claire. A plump rosy cheeked woman motioned to them as they entered the gallery.

"Sit yourselves down here. Coffee is it? And you'll be wanting a liqueur?"

"Coffee, yes, and I'll have a …" John hesitated.

"How about a Glayva or some of Bonnie Prince Charlie's secret brew … Drambuie?"

John agreed, and as the woman bustled away, he said "Told you, I knew he must have been here." Claire laughed "Alright, alright, I like this hotel, it is so comforting and popular, it is really busy."

"Yes indeed," John nodded looking around at the other guests. "I …"

"There you are," the elderly woman interrupted. "You'll sleep fine the night, with a good glass o' Drambuie inside you. The ghost will not bother you."

"Ghost?" Claire faltered.

"Aye, the chauffeur's son. He fell in love with Miss Clarissa, Lord Beaumont's daughter, aye, this was the family home, you see. She pointed to a portrait behind them. "That's Miss Clarissa, a bonnie lass." Claire turned and glanced at the portrait.

The woman babbled on. "well, she used to meet him in

the stables, but one night he didn't arrive. It was round about this time of the year. There had been a lot of rain in April and the burn was in spate. The weight of him and the horse and all the rain. He was washed away and drowned."

"Oh no. no." Claire gasped.

"Aye lassie, and there's some say they can hear the horse's hoof beats and some say that they have seen him. Every year on the anniversary of his death, he comes looking for Miss Clarissa, and he'll no rest till she comes back tae him. So don't go walking tonight this is his anniversary. I'll leave you before your coffee gets cold."

Claire had turned icy cool, her stomach was churning, she was going to be sick. "I'll be back" she gasped and ran out of the room. In her head she could hear his voice ... whispering.

She stood up, fighting the waves of nausea which threatened to overcome her. THIS WAS NOT HAPPENING. She was just overtired, stressed.

"Take deep breaths dear." It was the lady who had served coffee. "I saw you run out. I was like that with my first. It will pass. You'll be alright."

"But ... I'M NOT ... I'M NOT PREGNANT."

"Listen dear, I know the signs, but I am a stupid old woman upsetting you with my talk of ghosts."

"But ... is there a ghost? Is it true?"

"Och aye, but Andrew's a friendly ghost, only looking for his lost love. Tragedy all through the Beaumont family and scandal ... It was the women who caused the havoc." She stopped, "Are you alright now?"

"I ... yes, I'm feeling a little better. Tell me more." Claire's nausea had turned to a mixture of fear and excitement.

"Well, it started with Louise, the one who disgraced herself in India. Her parents brought her back, and promptly married her off to Lord Beaumont's youngest son. They seemed to be happy enough. She produced one daughter, then died in childbirth having the second. That was Miss Clarissa."

"At first Lord Beaumont doted on the girls, but as the years went on he blamed both of them for the death of their mother. When he found out about Andrew and Clarissa, he packed both girls off to stay with his sister in Gloucester. He died soon afterwards."

"And Clarissa, what happened to her?" Claire whispered.

"Oh now lassie, never you mind, half of it is aw made up for the tourists anyhow."

"What happened to her?" Claire repeated.

"Och well, she ... she died of a broken heart ... She drowned herself in her bath. That's the story, mind you I think there's a bit of a want wae aw the females in that family."

"What do you mean?" Claire whispered.

"A wee bit ... off" She pointed a finger at her head.

"Madness, you mean madness?"

"Well I suppose it was love, that caused it aw. That can drive us aw mad. Never you mind aw this talk, I ..."

Claire interrupted. "Louise, what about Louise, and her other daughter?"

"I don't know the full story, but that's why we have Sandalwood oil in the bathroom, Louise, the funeral pyre, you know, Och it's all for the tourists."

"And the other daughter?"

"I don't know about her dear."

"Away with you lassie, tell your husband the good news."

"Yes alright." Claire forced a smile. "Bye"

As she walked back into the Long Gallery, she saw John studying the portrait of Clarissa. He turned "There you are, are you alright?"

"Yes" she lied. "but it is a bit of a shock to look at this painting, she does look a bit like me."

"She does, she is even wearing a pendant like yours. Look!"

"Yes, so she is, my goodness ... Ummm, I'm a bit tired, can we go upstairs now?" She was fighting hard to keep control of herself.

"Alright, I wonder if Clarissa is one of your relatives, through the Bonnie Prince line." He laughed loudly.

He was still laughing as they climbed the stairs. As he turned the key in the lock, he said. "I better make a noise, if there are any ghosts that will scare them."

John fell asleep as soon as his head touched the pillow. Claire lay awake. Her heart was thudding, and her thoughts were chasing each other about her head. Louise ... the elderly lady had said. Louise ... could that have been? No., but her mother's middle name was Louise ...

It was unfortunate, but Claire and her mother had never been close, and she had only been in her late teens when her mother had died. Her mother had only once ... vaguely mentioned relatives ... in Scotland.

Relatives, oh, if only she had heard the rest of the conversation that day, when her mother and her aunty had been earnestly discussing someone's misdeeds.

Great Grandmother, Grandmother, Who? What? It was strange, that shortly after that conversation, her mother had to see a lawyer. When she returned, and Claire asked her about the visit, she mumbled something about worthless old jewellery.

Her mother never mentioned FAMILY and Claire thought it wise never to ask again. When her mother died, she left the pendant to Claire. The very drop pearl pendant Clarissa was wearing in the portrait. Don't be silly, Claire corrected herself, there must be hundreds like it.

What if? her thoughts persisted. What if? She sat up suddenly. HE WAS THERE AGAIN. She sprang out of bed and over to the window. The stable door, yes,.. the soft yellow light. Yes, HE WAS THERE, opening his arms to her. And in her head, he was whispering her name over and over, commanding her ...

She went to the dressing table, slid her hand under the dummy drawer. It clicked open, inside was a key. It fitted the door to the secret stairway.

The door creaked open, she looked over at John. He was out for the count till morning. She closed the door gently behind her and stood for a moment.

Chinks of light filtered through the gratings in the wall. She could just make out stone steps. She hesitated, panic sweeping over her. What was she doing? How did she know about this? The key? What?

He was whispering in her head again, whispering, whispering, commanding. She pushed her hand against the wall, and crept down the steps. As she reached the door at the bottom, it swung open.

She ran across to the stable and went inside. The yellow light was receding. There was nothing, or nobody there. She ran outside. In the distance, she could hear hoof beats.

"Andrew, wait for me, I'm coming to you." she shouted. She ran out of the courtyard and through the trees. He was guiding her now, in complete control of her, whispering.

She ran and stopped at the ancient burial mound. Moonlight bathed the grey stones in silver. Yes, it was all so familiar. She caught her breath, remembering what had been ...

He was whispering again. She must hurry. She must not be afraid. Suddenly clouds scudded across the moon. There was a loud crack of thunder, and lightning slashed across, inches from Claire's face.

She stood there, shaking as large spots of rain bounced on

to her, soaking her through. She turned, inching her way through bushes. The branches scratched her skin and tore her nightdress. Something wet and furry ran over her bare foot. She tripped over it and fell to the wet ground.

Andrew, she must get to him. She heard the sound of hoof beats, nearer and nearer. Soft yellow light, then the horseman. He was coming towards her, above her in the air. Reaching out to her, smiling, reaching. She felt herself floating upwards into his arms, out of time.

They found her next morning, in the stream, by the wooden bridge.

Emma sat up suddenly. She was shivering and the bed was freezing. She was gasping for breath and her heart was thumping. She reached out and snapped on the bedside lamp. She gulped and leaned back against the headboard. Would she ever be free from dreams of Steven?

Calm down, deep breaths, oh no, no. She fumbled for a cigarette and lit it. She inhaled deeply nearly choking. The dream pictures were still flashing through her mind.

The church in darkness, lit only by tall white candles. The sombre strains of the dead march wafting from the organ, and she, walking down the aisle alone.

Everything in white, her wedding dress dusted with tiny flowers like snowflakes. Her veil, scattered with frosted crystals and billowing out behind her in a cloud of tulle. Her bouquet, a simple posy of winter jasmine and waxy white lilies.

The congregation turning to look at her. Some of them wearing white wedding hats with veils over their white bones which had once been flesh. The others, they were all skeletons.

Suddenly they were all disappearing, and in their places, hundreds of white lilies, their sickly scent pervading the air. Somewhere far away, she heard a baby crying.

Now Steven was turning to look at her. He was wearing a white suit. His dark hair was plastered to his head in a frosty glittering halo.

His face was pure white, he had no eyes, just deep black sockets. His icy hands were tilting her face towards him. This was when she normally woke up, but tonight she had felt his kiss. His icy cold kiss.

She got up, pulled on her mother's dressing gown and lit another cigarette. Damm, I shouldn't be smoking she told herself. She filled her lungs with a few deep puffs and then stubbed the cigarette out in one of her mother's fancy little dishes.

She stared out of the window across the river to Kilcreggan. It was almost daylight now, cold and misty. She wondered if the little boatyard was still there, and if Steven's father still owned it.

Why? Why? Why? If only her father hadn't been such a bigot and a snob. What did it matter if Steven was a Catholic and she a Protestant. They had loved each other, but that wasn't good enough for her father, and her mother? She just did as her husband told her.

Tears slid down Emma's cheeks and she began to sob. She didn't hear her mother enter the room.

"I've brought you a cup of tea. You're crying. What's wrong? Are you ill?"

"No Mother I'm not ill ... thanks for the tea."

"Emma, it was a long time ago. Blue doesn't suit you dear, not with your nice dark hair and dark eyes."

"Mother, it may have been a long time ago, but I can't forget. It was all Father's fault."

"No need to shout Emma. You really must control yourself, or you'll make yourself ill again, and we don't want that do we?"

"No Mother we don't. Another mental breakdown m ... must be in the family, after all she should have got over it by now. My God, Mother, you're still terrified of what people think."

"Emma we hold a position in this town. Your father owns one of the most trusted law firms in the country. Now he's retiring, and he wants you to take charge. He's giving you his life's work. He did it all for you."

"So that's why I'm here. That's why you were so edgy last night. You're not ill at all are you?"

"No ... I knew you wouldn't come if your father asked you. He'll be home tomorrow night."

"He who must be obeyed at all costs. Position and money, that's all that matters, isn't it?"

"Emma your Father will be pleased to see you. He regrets what happened, but it's all in the past."

"Regrets? All in the past? No ... If Father had agreed to us being married, Steven would be alive today. I wouldn't have had a miscarriage, and you would have had a grandchild."

"But Emma, Steven was not what we wanted for you."

"Not what *you* wanted. You mean he wasn't in the professional class. Steven loved boats. He was training to be a marine engineer. His family liked me and I liked them. We were happy ... and our baby ... our poor baby."

"Emma, stop it ... It did matter. You were only eighteen and he was twenty-one. I suppose you thought it was love, whatever that is ... and the difference in religion."

"Mother ..."

"You have a good life in London, a good job. I don't approve of you living with Simon but if you marry him, and have children, that would be alright. You must have the son that I couldn't have. It would make your Father so happy."

"Oh Mother, just leave me alone ... *please.*"

Her Mother flounced out, banging the door behind her. Emma sighed and sat back in the big armchair. She tried to blink back the tears, but it was no use, she began to sob uncontrollably.

"Oh Steven," she whispered, her thoughts drifted back to the first time they had met each other. It had been at a Boat Club Saturday night hop. The place had been jammed with people and the trad jazz band had been belting it out. They had danced all night together and he had taken her home.

From that evening, they had seen each other at some time every day. Steven had taken her out in his little boat, which was really just a rowing boat with an outboard motor. He loved boats and the river.

She used to wait for him on the landing slip at the Boat Club. She would watch him as he sailed all the way across the river from Kilcreggan. As he drew nearer she could always see the yellow and blue flags fluttering at the stern.

When he landed, he would present the flags to her, and she would present him with a flower. It was so romantic. He was like The Lord of the Isles or a Viking Warrior coming to claim her as his bride.

They had been seeing each other for six months when they asked her father for permission to marry. Her father had raved and shouted and forbade her ever to see Steven again.

She had defied her Father and met Steven in secret. When she discovered that she was pregnant, they decided to elope.

"Oh Steven, Steven," she whispered. A sudden coldness invaded the room. She could hear his voice calling her name. She could see the grey green water boiling and spitting up angry foam. She could feel the wind cut through her hair with an icy comb. She was shaking with cold.

She could hear the thunder crashing among the hills and

she could see the lighting streaking the sky. She heard him shout "Emma. Emma."

She saw him vainly try to control the little boat, then it was all over. The wind had caught the boat, bouncing it from wave to wave till it capsized. She saw the river he loved claim him.

"Emma. Emma," her Mother was shaking her. "What are you starting at?"

"The storm."

"What are you talking about? Look it's calm, but there is a most peculiar looking mist. It must be really cold. Come downstairs and have some breakfast."

"Al .. right, but give me ten minutes."

Five minutes later Emma had washed and dressed. She went downstairs. She closed the outside door quietly behind her.

She walked down the drive, when she reached the large gates, she stopped. The winter jasmine growing against the wall was in bud and struggling to flower. She broke off a branch and stood smiling.

"Steven, oh Steven." He had once picked a branch from that same tree. He had handed it to her with a mocking bow, saying that it would forever remind him of her. It was small, fragile and very pretty and had to be loved or it wouldn't survive.

She closed the gates and crossed to the river side of the Esplanade. It was a bitterly cold March Morning, solid cold. She walked along looking neither right nor left, pausing only to wipe the water from her eyes and nose.

Two minutes later she reached the Boat Club. She made her way down the slippery steps by the side of it. She stood there on the shore, staring straight ahead.

The hills were hidden by a frozen curtain of grey white

mist that rose up from the river. The surface of the water seemed to boil and froth in the sub zero temperatures.

She spoke aloud, "Steven ... Steven. I know you can hear me. Come to me." She held out the branch of winter jasmine. In the distance, a voice ...

"Emmm ... mmaa ... Emmm ... mmaa."

His voice was becoming louder. A veil of mist was drifting towards her, drifting and swirling in a soft yellow light. The mist thinned and she could see the shadowy outline of a boat gliding through it.

The figure in the bow was holding a lantern and he was calling her. The boat came nearer and nearer, then suddenly stopped moving. It was too far from the shore.

The figure stood up and beckoned to her. "Emmm ... mmaa ... Emmm ... aa."

She walked into the water. She had to get to the boat, to him, to Steven. She was cold and the water was deep. She was gasping, just a little further. Oh, she was so cold, so heavy ... just a li ... ttle ...

Strong arms reached out and pulled her into the boat. She could smell the sweet scent of lilies and somewhere a baby was crying.

THE GREAT GARDEN FOUTER

Little silver trails glint in the early morning sun, and The Great Snail Hunter is on dawn patrol Armed only with a trusty garden cane he prods the cervices of our dry stone wall. And out tumbles delicately patterned molluscs who have gone to the great snail sanctuary.

They have been victims of the shake shake samba or snail shoogle and have been humanely killed by the tiny blue pellets that have been put down to form a defensive ring around plants and flowers.

It is not necessary to stamp on snails with a blood curdling crunch or leave them to the mercy of large birds who take them in their beaks and bash them to the ground.

However snails can play a might good game of hide and seek and often leave their gooey trails on the bait. Slugs too, seem to know how to avoid death food. According to scientists, grey slugs in particular appear to have a memory for odours and taste. So now you know.

A garden is a place frequented by many species. One of the most interesting is The Great Garden Fouter, instantly recognisable by his old togs and his habitual requests for coffee.

He keeps the garden in immaculate condition and rules over it with a will of iron. Yes he WILL give the grass another cut, even if it is still an inch high.

Pulling out anything that is not instantly recognisable is another form of tidying. Trying to convince him that it will grow again next year is not an easy task. Grudgingly he leaves it in place and pulls it out when I am not looking.

I think that Eve had an easier time in the Garden of Eden. After all she only had to tempt Adam with an apple and convince him that he didn't need his fig leaf.

A seeded area is a tit-bit for birds. It is fascinating to watch them as they peck mercilessly into the newly dug earth.

The G.G.F. stands at the window trying to scare the birds away by waving his arms about like a bookie at the races. When that doesn't work, he rushes out threatening to throttle them.

The birds fly off and return two minutes later to do the same thing all over again. It is a continual battle of wits in the Tom and Jerry mould. When the birds tire of that fun, they start foraging about among the bark chips sending them all over the place.

All these antics convince me that birds have bigger more active brains than we thought. Bees? Some of them have definite problems, otherwise why do they fly into a closed window knocking themselves out in the process?

I know that plants have feelings and that we should talk to them I DO but I am sure they wish they could talk to us. I can almost hear them scream in protest as the G.G.F. approaches them. *NOT ME AGAIN.*

No plant or flower is safe as the skulks about pruning,

cutting and moving. This is called forward planning. I call it horticultural murder as some plants appear to die of fright.

A visit to the local nursery for weed killer and NOTHING more, usually means the opposite. It is impossible to walk in, select the necessary item and walk out again.

A nursery is a place to FOUTER, and where togetherness blossoms and temptations are rife. It is so difficult to resist that pink camellia or that new purple rose.

Nature is a wonderful mystery and a garden is a magical place of changing seasons, colours and shapes. It can heal a troubled mind and calm a restless soul.

When The Great Garden Fouter sits down with me to enjoy a cuppa or a cool drink, sometimes we talk, sometimes we silently enjoy the peace and beauty around us.

Paradise on earth!

I can still hear that conversation as if it was yesterday, but it was twenty years ago. Now I am being asked to go to the funeral of the lady with the long yellow hair, Charlotte Victoria Barrington Smyth.

"Mummy can I be a tart when I grow up?"

"Elizabeth, what are you talking about? A tart is a cake, you know that."

"Yes Mummy, but Mrs Johnson was telling Mrs Brown that the lady with the yellow hair is a tart."

"Shhhh, Elizabeth, never use that word again about that lady. Do you hear me? Do you understand?"

"Yes Mummy." I didn't understand. Well I wouldn't. I was only six years old.

I couldn't see what all the fuss was about. The lady with the long yellow hair was beautiful. She wore red lipstick and her fingernails and toenails were painted red. She always smelt of perfume. According to Mrs Brown, expensive perfume that only a rich man would buy for a tart. I know that I should not have been listening to that gossip, so I did not tell Mummy.

I thought that the lady looked like a film star and if that was a tart then I wanted to be one when I grew up. She left the town suddenly and nothing more was heard of her. Most people thought that she had been killed in an air raid in London. If Mum knew where she was or what had happened she never told me. Now I am being asked to go to her funeral. Why me?

I suppose if Mum had been alive she would have gone because she liked her and often said she was a fine lady and did good work.

Mum did good work, so did all the ladies from the churches in the area. They ran a canteen for servicemen. It was on the main road near the Kings Theatre which was a picture house.

I just couldn't wait, the day Mum came to meet me at school. I had been told a secret, by one of the girls in my class. It was about Mrs Barrington Smyth, or the blonde tart, as she called her.

I breathlessly told my Mum all I had heard, that Mrs Barrington Smyth was called Bombay Sapphire. It was because she drank blue gin, and used to live in India, and had parties for men. She was so drunk sometimes that nobody saw her for two or three weeks. People were always talking about her.

Mum was very angry with me. She made me sit down and she lectured me that there was a war on, and if I was told a secret I must keep MUM. This meant I was not to tell anyone else, only her. Years later I was told that this was a Government slogan, and didn't really mean my mum.

If only Mum was here now, ohhh .. I miss her. If only I had known my Dad, but he was killed fighting in France. I was alone with Mum. My two brothers were evacuated to the Highlands but Mum thought that I was too young to be away from home.

Stop it! Stop it! Get on with it! My inner voice tells me Open the deed box and get on with it. Why are you hesitating? I go to the window and draw the curtains on a wet and windy night in Greenock.

It doesn't always rain here, it just seems like it does. I need a drink. I pour a healthy measure of Scotland's finest. Just a spot of water, mmm, that's good. Why does the first sip always taste better?

It seems so stupid it is frowned upon for a woman to drink whisky in public. Sherry is okay although James tells me that it is becoming popular with the ladies on the other side of the pond. When you come back from New York next I am going to drink whisky in public.

Oh stop it! Get on with it! Why me? Butterflies are going mad in my stomach. This is the way I felt years ago when I was very young. Air raids, screaming sirens, being dragged from my bed. Jostling into clothes, rushing to the shelter, then the all clear.

Then the real one, the biggie. The Blitz. Two nights of relentless pounding, continual drone of aircraft, the whine of landmines, the plop of explosions and bombs.

The Luftwaffe made a good job of it. They hit the power station at Dellingburn, the sugar refineries and the distillery. They were all blazed into oblivion. They gave the shipyards a hammering too. They were really what they were after. Thousands of people lost their homes and many more were killed.

Our neighbour Mr Gilchrist was killed in the raid. I remember Mum insisting that I go with her to pay our respects to him. There he was lying in a wooden box with his arms folded across his chest, asleep.

I remember thinking that when I lie in a wooden box I hope they remember to use Brasso when they polish the handles. Oh God is that all there is? I take a quick gulp of whisky. It goes down the wrong way, and I splutter and struggle to gain my breath.

I lift the letter and scan it again. Firm of lawyers London, imperative that I attend the funeral of Mrs Charlotte Victoria Barrington Smyth in London, details etc. Extremely important to go through all her papers before the funeral.

An appointment has been made for me with the Senior partner, regarding the will. What does this all mean? Why me? What is it all about?

I slide on to the floor and empty all the contents of the deed box on to the carpet. I lift a large envelope with a broken seal, printed on the front of it is:-

TO BE OPENED IN THE EVENT OF MY DEATH.

I, CHARLOTTE VICTORIA BARRINGTON SMYTH, WISH THE FOLLOWING ACCOUNT OF MY LIFE TO BE MADE KNOWN, WHEN THE TIME IS RIGHT, AND ONLY WHEN DEEMED NECESSARY. I ACCEPT THAT SPECIAL PERMISSION WILL BE NEEDED FROM THE POWERS THAT BE.

IT WAS SIGNED in large scrawly writing. My hands are shaking. The butterflies in my stomach are doing an eightsome reel. I pull out a sheaf of papers held together by two treasury tags. I begin to read.

MY DEAR LITTLE ONE,

I hardly know where to begin, but I hope and pray that when you read this you will understand and forgive me. I did what I had to do in the circumstances. There was a war on and life was very difficult.

I was born in Greenock, but when I was a toddler we moved to London, although we often came back to visit my aunt and uncle. My father worked in the Foreign Office. My mother stayed at home to look after myself and my brother.

Yes, I had been in India for a time when father was sent out there on duty. When we returned to London, my brother went up to Cambridge and I went to Cheltenham College for young ladies.

My brother was in his second year studies when he was recruited by the Secret Service. He was sent to the Continent on duty and died in a mysterious car crash.

I had lost a beloved brother, and much against my parents' wishes, I too joined the Intelligence Service. I was given a few menial tasks that were perfectly safe. Then one day I was asked if I would consider a more dangerous job. I said yes.

I was sent to Greenock and set up in a big house in Octavia Terrace in the west end of town. I was to play Lady Bountiful with Black Market contacts and a dubious reputation. I was to be a drunken slut who always dressed in sapphire blue to match the gin bottle. I was back home to make money.

In the weeks that I was supposed to be on a bender I was on special duty, usually in France with the Resistance. It was there that I fell in love with Jean Luc and you my little one were the result.

Jean Luc never knew about you. When I finally realised that I was pregnant and told my superiors I was whisked off to the country out of the way.

When you were born you were taken away from me immediately. I never saw you. I was told it was a girl. I was so depressed. It was so cruel to take you away. I pleaded with them. I was told that there was a war on, and we all had to make sacrifices.

I had a job to do and I did it. I had to. Jean Luc had been killed. I had no child. I had nothing left. I did what I had to do. They promised me that you would be well looked after, and when the war was all over we would be together.

I was too valuable to them. I had all the skills required. They kept you near me, so that if I did not carry out my assignments, you could be used against me. Such are the powers of emotional blackmail.

I never knew where you were, but the first time I saw you with Jane, I knew. You had Jean Luc's dark eyes and his dark curly hair. I knew. I just knew. But I could do nothing.

Jane had two sons who were evacuated up North as soon as the war became imminent. Her husband signed on for the navy. The boat he was on was sunk by a U boat. Jane worked at the torpedo factory and was recruited from there.

She wasn't told who you really were but she knew that you were a child of one of the many girls who worked in the espionage trade.

I could never ask you or tell you what I suspected. I could never ask Jane. I could never ask anyone. It was all too dangerous. You could have been kidnapped. I could have been held to ransom. Neither Jean Luc or my parents knew about you.

A few months before the war ended I was sent to the north of Scotland with many others whose cover was blown by treachery.

When it was safe they let me out. They told me that you had died of T.B. and that I would just have to get on with it, to forget everything and be normal again. Normal?

How could I ever be normal again? I still had to take precautions. I had to change my looks and my name. They wouldn't even tell me where you were buried.

I was desolate. I had no child, no Jean Luc, and my parents had been killed in an air raid. I had nothing. I was taken back to London and given a menial job in a Government office.

I was contacted by someone I once knew. He told me that you were alive. I won't go into details because he is well known and had friends in high places. He told me all about you and even managed to get me a photograph of you.

Forgive me my daughter. I could not come back from the dead. I could not wreck your life. Forgive me. I did what I had to do. Never a day passed when I did not think of you. I am sorry that you have to find out like this. I did not desert you. Forgive me, but I had to do what I did.

They promised me that this letter, plus all the other bits and pieces would be passed to you, and at least you could attend my funeral ... Be happy. Think of me in a kind way.

Your loving mother.

ASHES TO ASHES, dust to dust. I throw a red rose into the black hole where my mother lies, in that wooden box with the shiny brass handles.

THE TEARS START AGAIN.

THE REFORMATION

"Be sure your sins will find you out," thundered Andrew from the pulpit. Elizabeth sighed, oh no, not again. What is it with him? All this fire and brimstone, it is just not Andrew. She looked at her watch, Oh God it was going to be another half hour sermon. She really would have to talk to him.

He was becoming more straight laced than John Knox and twice as boring. In that split second, she made up her mind. She needed a break, so she would spend the week-end with Jill. It would be fun and she would find out the secret that Jill would not reveal over the phone.

She looked up at her husband. How did she ever become first lady of this very prestigious manse in Morningside? They had been very lucky. It had been Andrew's first charge and they had been an enthusiastic young couple who set out to make the world a better place. Now, something was going badly wrong with their life. She resented having to take sides between her sixteen year old son and her husband. She felt at times a non person, only existing as the minister's wife or her son's mother. She jumped as the organist crashed into the chords of the closing hymn. Fight the good Fight. How appropriate!

She stood at the church door with her husband, shaking hands and saying all the right things. She cringed inwardly as John K. Livingstone squeezed her hand and stepped closer. She didn't like this big blustering man with the stark white hair and moustache but she had to admit that he did a lot of work for the church. Rumours were rife about his womanising but Andrew liked him, said he was all talk and as a prominent member of the legal fraternity he couldn't possibly be involved in anything like that. Andrew used to joke that she was the reason that more men accompanied their wives to church. Now he complained that her skirt was too short, her blonde hair was dyed. She didn't look like a minister's wife and she spent too much time on the computer. She had protested that she was part of the modernisation of the church and he had approved of it, and so had the members of the church.

At last they escaped to the car and made their way home. Elizabeth busied herself with lunch as Andrew droned on and on about Duncan's shortcomings, and were they wise to have let him go to Australia on holiday.

Elizabeth said yes and no, nodded and shook her head at the right time, then she casually said "Andrew, I'm going to Glasgow on Friday, Jill has asked me through for the weekend. She's going on line and wants my help."

"The week-end? You have never discussed it with me."

"I mentioned it but you weren't listening."

"But you saw her two months ago."

"Yes, but that was our usual meeting for lunch."

"Well I hope that you will be back in time for church on Sunday."

Friday came and Elizabeth went. Andrew didn't even kiss her good-bye at the station.

As she sat on the train gazing out of the window and not really looking at anything she vaguely wondered if she should have kicked over the traces more before she had settled down.

She had been married at twenty and had produced Duncan ten months later. She and Andrew were happy, but every now and then he would ask her if he was too dull for her. She always said No, but that was then, and she enjoyed being wrapped in their own private cocoon of respectability.

Andrew was a quiet man and that was what attracted her to him. They were total opposites. The first few years of their marriage had been such a struggle, even with her part time job working from home.

However when Andrew qualified and they moved from his poky flat in Glasgow to this manse life became Heaven on earth.

She still envied Jill a little because she was her own person and did exactly as she wanted. She travelled the world in search of rare books to fill the little bookshop which she owned.

She and Elizabeth had always got on well together and remained close friends telling each other all their innermost secrets, but, what was this new secret?

Jill had a sense of the dramatic, so perhaps she was getting married after all. No. She sounded different about this, and said that it was an idea that Jonathan had though about.

He was her long time boyfriend, a handsome man divorced three times with two grown up children. He was also a member of the legal establishment.

The train stopped and brought Elizabeth into a cloudy grey Glasgow. Jill came running up the platform to welcome her.

"Hello, I know. You're desperate to know, but I can't tell

you here. All I can say, is that you will believe it. You will be amused and you should be shocked, you being a Minister's wife."

"Well, what can I say? I'm speechless."

They both burst into gales of laughter then Jill suddenly became serious. "When I tell you this, you must never reveal it to anyone, not even Andrew, especially not Andrew."

They went straight to Jill's flat and settled down to a large pot of tea and a plate of mini jam doughnuts.

"Well, go on. Tell all. You're not going to get married are you?"

"Heavens no," she laughed, "sorry about the holy reference. Tell me about you first. You sounded a bit down when I phoned. Tell Auntie Jill."

"Well, Andrew's going on a bit, Duncan is playing up and I'm stuck in the middle."

"Life! Jonathan can be a perfect swine but that's part of the fun isn't it? Would be very boring if we were on cloud nine all the time."

"I know. Anyway I can't wait any longer. Tell or I'll scream."

"We-ell. Are you sitting comfortably? Now I'll begin."

"Well?"

"I have entered a profession."

"What profession?"

"The most famous one in the world, and the oldest."

"What? Jill, what do you mean?"

"I mean I am going to be a Madame." She started to giggle. "You should see your face Elizabeth."

"You're serious."

"YES. Jonathan and a few of his friends bought the Hen House last year. We've been in operation for three months."

"The Hen House? You mean, a brothel."

"Please, a House of Pleasure."

Both of them started to giggle. Jill held up her hand. "Just listen, and Madame will tell you all."

Elizabeth was fascinated as Jill calmly explained. It was really a private club for gentlemen. It had a small intimate restaurant and health facilities.

It was only for invited members and it was very up market. The ladies were all from good families and medically sound. The gentlemen were all from the professions, including the clergy.

"When the General Assembly was in session, the ladies had a busy time." Jill said jokingly.

Elizabeth retorted, "I find that hard to believe."

"Don't worry I haven't seen Andrew yet."

"That is not funny."

"Sorry."

"Where is this place?"

"In the country, half way between Glasgow and Edinburgh, very convenient."

"But what if someone tells?"

"Not possible, Jonathan vets the clientele very carefully, besides it's a private club with a first class restaurant. The .. eh .. facilities .. health facilities, are optional."

"The Hen House?"

"Yes. Think Glasgow vernacular."

"Of course." They both started to laugh.

"Oh Jill, well that's one place where credit card rating will have a new meaning. And do they use other names?"

"Some do but I told you it's all very hush hush. I want your help."

"UHHuh. Going on line at the shop."

"That was just an excuse. It's all on line. The Hen House, ummm, do you think you might? I need someone who can keep a secret."

"We-ell I can certainly do that. I have to. Mmm, could add a bit of spice to my life. Why not?"

They spent the rest of the time eating, drinking and making plans.

On the train home Elizabeth was deep in thought. She kept sniggering aloud to herself at the very thought. What a secret. What fun.

Andrew was at the station to meet her but he was in a sullen mood and didn't even ask her if she had enjoyed the week-end. He only greeted her with a catalogue of woes.

Over supper she found it hard to keep her temper. He had to stop worrying about everything. He was doing his best and he was succeeding, but he was becoming a sort of ecclesiastical Braveheart. He worried for Scotland saying that another Reformation was needed.

Yes, she thought, a Reformation in our marriage. She tried to make allowances for the fact that his fortieth birthday loomed large. And tried to laugh it off when he had looked at her with his dark brooding eyes and asked her if she had noticed that his dark hair was going white at the temples.

She feigned an excuse and went to bed early. She sighed. She was looking forward to her new position. She giggled, if that was the correct word. She fell asleep cuddling her secret.

Next morning she told Andrew that from now on she would be away every week-end, and YES, she would return in time for church on Sunday morning.

The following week-end there she was wearing a black wig, a discreet black dress and pearls, sitting in a curtained alcove behind an antique desk and calling herself Madame Anastasia.

As Jill said, what was sin anyway? A transgression to some, a pleasure to others. The doorbell chimed and Madame rose from her gilded chair.

Six weeks later Elizabeth was getting used to this new pattern in her life. It amused her that some clients often made appointments under a variety of assumed names.

There were weekly visits from Napoleon Bonaparte, Rabbie Burns and Dr. Crippen. She loved to guess who the men really were and what they did for a living.

One Friday evening she became intrigued to know who Julius Caesar and the four members of the Senate might be. Promptly at eight o'clock they appeared, led by John K. Livingstone who boomed at her "The Emperor Caesar and friends."

She nearly fainted as he leaned closer to her and whispered "What a hoot. Church of Old Scotia minister with us for a meal. Doesn't know what other pleasures await him. Well poor sod. Fortieth birthday next week. Give him a treat."

Elizabeth managed a taut smile then returned to the others and could not believe that one of them was her husband. Her lips were quivering now and she was shaking as she led them to the foot of the stairs.

She sat down. Her heat was jumping and thumping in her chest. She felt sick as the full enormity of what she was doing hit her like a juggernaut.

Andrew. He didn't look as if he had been dragged in here kicking and screaming. She tried to steady herself as she lifted the phone and dialled Jill's number.

On Saturday afternoon Andrew was at the station as usual to meet her. She greeted him nervously, but he floored her by telling her that John K. Livingstone had died suddenly. He refused to say anymore till they got home.

Then he told her the circumstances and admitted that he had been there in the Gentlemen's Club. He was shocked into disbelief when she told him that she had seen him.

He had not recognised her and he kept asking if this was a

joke. There was a terrible row and Andrew stomped off to sleep in one of the guest bedrooms.

A few days later, there was a lovely funeral. Andrew announced the merits of John's life, and the fact that he had remained active right up to the end, but unfortunately the vigorous exercise at his health club, had brought on a heart attack.

None of the congregation knew the true story, but they all had their suspicions which were fuelled into flames when they noticed the two pews at the back of the church were filled by smartly dressed women wearing black.

Elizabeth never knew whether Andrew had indulged in the pleasures of the Hen House. Andrew never knew if Elizabeth had ever gratified her wildest desires.

Life at the manse was very awkward for a few months. Neither of them dared to ask the other, so the matter was dropped.

Andrew returned to the marital bed, but relations were strained and would take some time to return to normal.

However, it is enough to say that on one particular Sunday morning when Andrew stood in the pulpit looking down on his wife, she smiled when he began his sermon.

"Let he that is without sin among you. Let him first cast a stone."

TRAFFIC CONE SYNDROME

They are at it again, multiplying all over the country. Armies of them in red and white uniforms rule with military precision. Traffic cones are in charge of our roads and motorways.

There they stand, looking at us with that smug superior expression, as if to say, you must obey us whether you like it or not.

Are they a ploy of a foreign government, or a power from another planet? Perhaps someone, somewhere is conducting a 'Clone a Cone' study or experiment? Could this even be part of a more sinister plan to drive the motorist completely off the road?

What can we do about them? Why not be friendly towards them, show a little kindness? Poor things remain in position day and night, enduring their allowance of noxious fumes and the hatred of all road users.

We could start by painting them with the emblems, flags and tartan of our separate nations. We could then organise a traffic cone treasure hunt for children.

Finding tartan, thistles, roses or leeks among cones on

selected roads might keep them from becoming bored. This might also stop the all too familiar question and answer session which usually concerns the time of the journey and having to "go" again.

What about a Cone Club for children? They could have fun whilst learning about the highway code and the dangers of traffic. They might even enjoy wearing baseball caps, badges or T-shirts proclaiming, TRAFFIC CONES ARE COOL.

Lands' End could perhaps fund a new line for adults, with a discreet cone logo on the pocket of a polo shirt?

A national 'Hug a Cone for Charity' day might be an idea. Buy a cone doll, cone teddy or cone worry beads. This may amuse motorists and help them to keep their temper and blood pressure under control as they are forced through yet another chicane of cones.

The medics might approve, with the thought that this is a new version of 'Love your Enemy it's good for your Health'.

Would cones be more appealing if they had flowers sprouting from them? The motorways could then compete with each other for the Charlie Dimmock trophy for the Best Kept Garden Motorway. Service stations could be encouraged, where possible, to provide a garden area for angst ridden motorists to stroll around and hopefully find a little calm before returning to the race tracks that are our motorways.

Art Nouveau may even flourish as trendies make fashion statements. Diamonds and cut glass jewellery would flash like traffic lights as earrings and body ornaments.

Kitchen utensils, cone shaped mugs, cutlery very modern, very stylish. In fact, any room in the house, could have a tiny object shaped like a cone. All in an effort to help us cope with cones.

Furniture designers would be influenced by the conical shape and would use it in everything from lamps to beds.

The confectionary trade would accept the challenge with cone shaped chocolates, even cone rock with the names of towns or motorway numbers stamped through it.

Ice cream cones, in raspberry and white stripes of course. A new version of the old favourite Knickerbocker Glory, that would make the original pale into insignificance.

TV chefs would create all manner of new dishes, like coneburger and chips, cone cod fish fingers. And for the gourmet, a delicate blend of seafood in white wine, piled up in shape, all ready to fall over your plate the instant that you touch it with your cutlery.

Cocktails would become popular again with names like Cosmic Cone, to make you 'lift off' into space. Vodka Venus speaks for itself. And if you dare to drink Motorway Madness or Road Rage then you are going to have a concrete headache.

In the music world, perhaps a new group, The Conettes. A new dance, Cone Conga, where people weave their way in and out through lines of cones.

Traffic Cone Syndrome or Conitis will become the fashionable illness of the future, responsible for all ailments from backache to divorce.

What is a cone hotline? Is it for stressed out cones or agitated and worried motorists who start to see red and white dwarves with pointed heads?

It is worth remembering that today's cones are tomorrow's antiques, so start collecting now, before they become illegal and are replaced by super efficient Euro cones.

It is grudgingly accepted that cones have to be used to control the traffic, but do they have to make their presence felt on almost every road in the country?

What happens to the older generation of cones? Do they end up on the eternal motorway in the sky, on duty at the heavenly gates, to separate the saints from the sinners?

You can bet on it!